# the GOLDEN KEY

# the GOLDEN KEY

## AND OTHER STORIES

### BY
# GEORGE MACDONALD

## ILLUSTRATED
### BY
# CRAIG YOE

WM. B. EERDMANS PUBLISHING CO.

# CONTENTS

## ILLUSTRATIONS

The story-title decoration is based on an anagram George MacDonald invented from the letters of his name. It was adopted as a family emblem.

## PUBLISHER'S NOTE

"**I**T must be more than thirty years ago that I bought . . . *Phantastes*. A few hours later I knew I had crossed a great frontier. . . . What it actually did to me was to convert, even to baptise, my imagination."

In those words C. S. Lewis, creator of the Narnia Chronicles, reported his discovery of George MacDonald, one of the nineteenth-century innovators of modern fantasy. Thanks in part to Lewis's appreciation—"I regarded him as my master"—MacDonald came to influence not only Lewis himself but that circle of Lewis's friends in Oxford who called themselves the Inklings. Included were Charles Williams and—more famously—J. R. R. Tolkien, who has paid his own tribute to the "power and beauty" of MacDonald's accomplishment.

George MacDonald was born in 1824, five years later than Queen Victoria; he died four years after her, in 1905. His birthplace was Huntly, Aberdeenshire, in Northwest Scotland, and his Scottish background shows through his work, in its kindly but unsentimental astringency and its love of the commonplace, even more clearly than does the Victorian world in which he later moved as a resident of London. In 1840 he entered Kings College at Aberdeen, and ten years later he became clergyman to a chapel at Arundel, a position he left in 1853 to begin what was to be a long career as highly respected writer, lecturer, and preacher. Among his literary friends were Carlyle, Tennyson, William Morris, and Lewis Carroll. In 1872 he travelled on a spectacularly successful lecture tour of the United States, where he was hailed by the popular press and saw such prominent men of letters as Whittier and Emerson.

MacDonald wrote a number of conventional Victorian novels, modestly successful in his own time but of interest now largely as period pieces. It is for his entrancing fantasy that MacDonald is justly revered today by an enthusiastic and growing readership. These fantasy works include the adult "Faerie Romances" *Phantastes* and *Lilith* and three full-length children's classics: *At the Back of the North Wind, The Princess and the Goblin*, and *The Princess and Curdie*.

Much of MacDonald's best fantasy writing, however, is found in his shorter stories, which in his lifetime were published in such collections as *Adela Cathcart* (1864) and *The Gifts of the Child Christ, and Other Tales* (1882). In the present volume and its companion volumes in THE FANTASY STORIES OF GEORGE MACDONALD, editor Glenn Sadler has compiled a complete edition of MacDonald's shorter works, newly illustrated by artists Craig and Janet Yoe.

"I do not write," MacDonald once said, "for children, but for the childlike, whether of five, or fifty, or seventy-five." Here, then, for the childlike of all ages, is a collection of fairy tales and stories certain to delight both confirmed MacDonald readers and those about to meet him for the first time.

# THE GOLDEN KEY

HERE was a boy who used to sit in the twilight and listen to his great-aunt's stories.

She told him that if he could reach the place where the end of the rainbow stands he would find there a golden key.

"And what is the key for?" the boy would ask. "What is it the key of? What will it open?"

"That nobody knows," his aunt would reply. "He has to find that out."

"I suppose, being gold," the boy once said, thoughtfully, "that I could get a good deal of money for it if I sold it."

"Better never find it than sell it," returned his aunt.

And then the boy went to bed and dreamed about the golden key.

Now all that his great-aunt told the boy about the golden key would have been nonsense, had it not been that their little house stood on the borders of Fairyland. For it is perfectly well known that out of Fairyland nobody ever can find where the rainbow stands. The creature takes such good care of its golden key, always flitting from place to place, lest anyone should find it! But in Fairyland it is quite different. Things that look real in this country look very thin indeed in Fairyland, while some of the things that here cannot stand still for a moment, will not move

Reprinted from *Dealings with Fairies* (1867).

there. So it was not in the least absurd of the old lady to tell her nephew such things about the golden key.

"Did you ever know anybody find it?" he asked, one evening.

"Yes. Your father, I believe, found it."

"And what did he do with it, can you tell me?"

"He never told me."

"What was it like?"

"He never showed it to me."

"How does a new key come there always?"

"I don't know. There it is."

"Perhaps it is the rainbow's egg."

"Perhaps it is. You will be a happy boy if you find the nest."

"Perhaps it comes tumbling down the rainbow from the sky."

"Perhaps it does."

One evening, in summer, he went into his own room, and stood at the lattice-window, and gazed into the forest which fringed the outskirts of Fairyland. It came close up to his great-aunt's garden, and, indeed, sent some straggling trees into it. The forest lay to the east, and the sun, which was setting behind the cottage, looked straight into the dark wood with his level red eye. The trees were all old, and had few branches below, so that the sun could see a great way into the forest; and the boy, being keen-sighted, could see almost as far as the sun. The trunks stood like rows of red columns in the shine of the red sun, and he could see down aisle after aisle in the vanishing distance. And as he gazed into the forest he began to feel as if the trees were all waiting for him, and had something they could not go on with till he came to them. But he was hungry, and wanted his supper. So he lingered.

Suddenly, far among the trees, as far as the sun could shine, he saw a glorious thing. It was the end of a rainbow, large and brilliant. He could count all the seven colours, and could see shade after shade beyond the violet; while before the red stood a colour more gorgeous and mysterious still. It was a colour he had never seen before. Only the spring of the rainbow-arch was visible. He could see nothing of it above the trees.

"The golden key!" he said to himself, and darted out of the house, and into the wood.

He had not gone far before the sun set. But the rainbow only glowed the brighter. For the rainbow of Fairyland is not dependent upon the sun as ours is. The trees welcomed him. The bushes made way for him. The rainbow grew larger and brighter; and at length he found himself within two trees of it.

It was a grand sight, burning away there in silence, with its gorgeous, its lovely, its delicate colours, each distinct, all combining. He could now see a great deal more of it. It rose high into the blue heavens, but bent so little that he could not tell how high the crown of the arch must reach. It was still only a small portion of a huge bow.

He stood gazing at it till he forgot himself with delight—even forgot the key which he had come to seek. And as he stood it grew more wonderful still. For in each of the colours, which was as large as the column of a church, he could faintly see beautiful forms slowly ascending as if by the steps of a winding stair. The forms appeared irregularly—now one, now many, now several, now none—men and women and children—all different, all beautiful.

He drew nearer to the rainbow. It vanished. He started back a step in dismay. It was there again, as beautiful as ever. So he contented himself with standing as near it as he might, and watching the forms that ascended the glorious colours towards the unknown height of the arch, which did not end abruptly,

3

but faded away in the blue air, so gradually that he could not say where it ceased.

When the thought of the golden key returned, the boy very wisely proceeded to mark out in his mind the space covered by the foundation of the rainbow, in order that he might know where to search, should the rainbow disappear. It was based chiefly upon a bed of moss.

Meantime it had grown quite dark in the wood. The rainbow alone was visible by its own light. But the moment the moon rose the rainbow vanished. Nor could any change of place restore the vision to the boy's eyes. So he threw himself down upon the mossy bed, to wait till the sunlight would give him a chance of finding the key. There he fell fast asleep.

When he woke in the morning the sun was looking straight into his eyes. He turned away from it, and the same moment saw a brilliant little thing lying on the moss within a foot of his face. It was the golden key. The pipe of it was of plain gold, as bright as gold could be. The handle was curiously wrought and set with sapphires. In a terror of delight he put out his hand and took it, and had it.

He lay for a while, turning it over and over, and feeding his eyes upon its beauty. Then he jumped to his feet, remembering that the pretty thing was of no use to him yet. Where was the lock to which the key belonged? It must be somewhere, for how could anybody be so silly as make a key for which there was no lock? Where should he go to look for it? He gazed about him, up into the air, down to the earth, but saw no keyhole in the clouds, in the grass, or in the trees.

Just as he began to grow disconsolate, however, he saw something glimmering in the wood. It was a mere glimmer that he saw, but he took it for a glimmer of rainbow, and went towards it.—And now I will go back to the borders of the forest.

Not far from the house where the boy had lived, there was another house, the owner of which was a merchant, who was much away from home. He had lost his wife some years before, and had only one child, a little girl, whom he left to the charge of two servants, who were very idle and careless. So she was neglected and left untidy, and was sometimes ill-used besides.

Now it is well known that the little creatures commonly called fairies, though there are many different kinds of fairies in Fairyland, have an exceeding dislike to untidiness. Indeed, they are quite spiteful to slovenly people. Being used to all the lovely ways of the trees and flowers, and to the neatness of the birds and all woodland creatures, it makes them feel miserable, even in their deep woods and on their grassy carpets, to think that within the same moonlight lies a dirty, uncomfortable, slovenly house. And this makes them angry with the people that live in it, and they would gladly drive them out of the world if they could. They want the whole earth nice and clean. So they pinch the maids black and blue, and play them all manner of uncomfortable tricks.

But this house was quite a shame, and the fairies in the forest could not endure it. They tried everything on the maids without effect, and at last resolved upon making a clean riddance, beginning with the child. They ought to have known that it was not her fault, but they have little principle and much mischief in them, and they thought that if they got rid of her the maids would be sure to be turned away.

So one evening, the poor little girl having been put to bed early, before the sun was down, the servants went off to the village, locking the door behind them. The child did not know she was alone, and lay con-

tentedly looking out of her window towards the forest, of which, however, she could not see much,
because of the ivy and other creeping plants which
had straggled across her window. All at once she saw
an ape making faces at her out of the mirror, and the
heads carved upon a great old wardrobe grinning fear-
fully. Then two old spider-legged chairs came forward
into the middle of the room, and began to dance a
queer, old-fashioned dance. This set her laughing,
and she forgot the ape and the grinning heads. So the
fairies saw they had made a mistake, and sent the
chairs back to their places. But they knew that she
had been reading the story of Silverhair all day. So
the next moment she heard the voices of the three
bears upon the stair, big voice, middle voice, and little
voice, and she heard their soft, heavy tread, as if they
had had stockings over their boots, coming nearer
and nearer to the door of her room, till she could bear
it no longer. She did just as Silverhair did, and as the
fairies wanted her to do: she darted to the window,
pulled it open, got upon the ivy, and so scrambled to
the ground. She then fled to the forest as fast as she
could run.

Now, although she did not know it, this was the
very best way she could have gone; for nothing is
ever so mischievous in its own place as it is out of
it; and, besides, these mischievous creatures were
only the children of Fairyland, as it were, and there
are many other beings there as well; and if a wanderer
gets in among them, the good ones will always help
him more than the evil ones will be able to hurt him.

The sun was now set, and the darkness coming
on, but the child thought of no danger but the bears
behind her. If she had looked round, however, she
would have seen that she was followed by a very different creature from a bear. It was a curious creature,
made like a fish, but covered, instead of scales, with

feathers of all colours, sparkling like those of a hum-ming-bird. It had fins, not wings, and swam through the air as a fish does through the water. Its head was like the head of a small owl.

After running a long way, and as the last of the light was disappearing, she passed under a tree with drooping branches. It dropped its branches to the ground all about her, and caught her as in a trap. She struggled to get out, but the branches pressed her closer and closer to the trunk. She was in great terror and distress, when the air-fish, swimming into the thicket of branches, began tearing them with its beak. They loosened their hold at once, and the creature went on attacking them, till at length they let the child go. Then the air-fish came from behind her, and swam on in front, glittering and sparkling all lovely colours; and she followed.

It led her gently along till all at once it swam in at a cottage-door. The child followed still. There was a bright fire in the middle of the floor, upon which stood a pot without a lid, full of water that boiled and bub-bled furiously. The air-fish swam straight to the pot and into the boiling water, where it lay quietly. A beautiful woman rose from the opposite side of the fire and came to meet the girl. She took her up in her arms, and said,—

"Ah, you are come at last! I have been looking for you a long time."

She sat down with her on her lap, and there the girl sat staring at her. She had never seen anything so beautiful. She was tall and strong, with white arms and neck, and a delicate flush on her face. The child could not tell what was the colour of her hair, but could not help thinking it had a tinge of dark green. She had not one ornament upon her, but she looked as if she had just put off quantities of diamonds and emeralds. Yet here she was in the simplest, poorest little cottage, where she was evidently at home. She was dressed in shining green.

The girl looked at the lady, and the lady looked at the girl.

"What is your name?" asked the lady.

"The servants always called me Tangle."

"Ah, that was because your hair was so untidy. But that was their fault, the naughty women! Still it is a pretty name, and I will call you Tangle too. You must not mind me asking you questions, for you may ask me the same questions, every one of them, and any others that you like. How old are you?"

"Ten," answered Tangle.

"You don't look like it," said the lady.

"How old are you, please?" returned Tangle.

"Thousands of years old," answered the lady.

"You don't look like it," said Tangle.

"Don't I? I think I do. Don't you see how beautiful I am?"

And her great blue eyes looked down on the little Tangle, as if all the stars in the sky were melted in them to make their brightness.

Ah! but," said Tangle, "when people live long they grow old. At least I always thought so."

"I have no time to grow old," said the lady. "I am too busy for that. It is very idle to grow old.—But I cannot have my little girl so untidy. Do you know I can't find a clean spot on your face to kiss?"

"Perhaps," suggested Tangle, feeling ashamed, but not too much so to say a word for herself—"perhaps that is because the tree made me cry so."

"My poor darling!" said the lady, looking now as if the moon were melted in her eyes, and kissing her little face, dirty as it was, "the naughty tree must suffer for making a girl cry."

"And what is your name, please?" asked Tangle.

"Grandmother," answered the lady.

"Is it really?"

"Yes, indeed. I never tell stories, even in fun."

"How good of you!"

"I couldn't if I tried. It would come true if I said it, and then I should be punished enough."

And she smiled like the sun through a summer-shower.

"But now," she went on, "I must get you washed and dressed, and then we shall have some supper."

"Oh! I had supper long ago," said Tangle.

"Yes, indeed you had," answered the lady—"three years ago. You don't know that it is three years since you ran away from the bears. You are thirteen and more now."

Tangle could only stare. She felt quite sure it was true.

"You will not be afraid of anything I do with you—will you?" said the lady.

"I will try very hard not to be; but I can't be certain, you know," replied Tangle.

"I like your saying so, and I shall be quite satisfied," answered the lady.

She took off the girl's night-gown, rose with her in her arms and going to the wall of the cottage, opened a door. Then Tangle saw a deep tank, the sides of which were filled with green plants, which had flowers of all colours. There was a roof over it like the roof of the cottage. It was filled with beautiful clear water, in which swam a multitude of such fishes as the one that had led her to the cottage. It was the light their colours gave that showed the place in which they were.

The lady spoke some words Tangle could not understand, and threw her into the tank.

The fishes came crowding about her. Two or three of them got under her head and kept it up. The rest of them rubbed themselves all over her, and with their

9

wet feathers washed her quite clean. Then the lady, who had been looking on all the time, spoke again; whereupon some thirty or forty of the fishes rose out of the water underneath Tangle, and so bore her up to the arms the lady held out to her. She carried her back to the fire, and, having dried her well, opened a chest, and taking out the finest linen garments, smelling of grass and lavender, put them upon her, and over all a green dress, just like her own, shining like hers, and soft like hers, and going into just such lovely folds from the waist, where it was tied with a brown cord, to her bare feet.

"Won't you give me a pair of shoes too, Grandmother?" said Tangle.

"No, my dear; no shoes. Look here. I wear no shoes."

So saying, she lifted her dress a little, and there were the loveliest white feet, but no shoes. Then Tangle was content to go without shoes too. And the lady sat down with her again, and combed her hair, and brushed it, and then left it to dry while she got the supper.

First she got bread out of one hole in the wall; then milk out of another; then several kinds of fruit out of a third; and then she went to the pot on the fire, and took out the fish, now nicely cooked, and, as soon as she had pulled off its feathered skin, ready to be eaten.

"But," exclaimed Tangle. And she stared at the fish, and could say no more.

"I know what you mean," returned the lady. "You do not like to eat the messenger that brought you home. But it is the kindest return you can make. The creature was afraid to go until it saw me put the pot on, and heard me promise it should be boiled the moment it returned with you. Then it darted out of the door at once. You saw it go into the pot of itself the moment it entered, did you not?"

"I did," answered Tangle, "and I thought it very strange; but then I saw you, and forgot all about the fish."

"In Fairyland," resumed the lady, as they sat down to the table, "the ambition of the animals is to be eaten by the people; for that is their highest end in that condition. But they are not therefore destroyed. Out of that pot comes something more than the dead fish, you will see."

Tangle now remarked that the lid was on the pot. But the lady took no further notice of it till they had eaten the fish, which Tangle found nicer than any fish she had ever tasted before. It was as white as snow, and as delicate as cream. And the moment she had swallowed a mouthful of it, a change she could not describe began to take place in her. She heard a murmuring all about her, which became more and more articulate, and at length, as she went on eating, grew intelligible. By the time she had finished her share, the sounds of all the animals in the forest came crowding through the door to her ears; for the door still stood wide open, though it was pitch dark outside; and they were no longer sounds only; they were speech, and speech that she could understand. She could tell what the insects in the cottage were saying to each other too. She had even a suspicion that the trees and flowers all about the cottage were holding midnight communications with each other; but what they said she could not hear.

As soon as the fish was eaten, the lady went to the fire and took the lid off the pot. A lovely little creature in human shape, with large white wings, rose out of it, and flew round and round the roof of the cottage; then dropped, fluttering, and nestled in the lap of the lady. She spoke to it some strange words, carried it to the door, and threw it out into the darkness. Tangle heard the flapping of its wings die away in the distance.

"Now have we done the fish any harm?" she said, returning.

"No," answered Tangle, "I do not think we have. I should not mind eating one every day."

"They must wait their time, like you and me too, my Tangle."

And she smiled a smile which the sadness in it made more lovely.

"But," she continued, "I think we may have one for supper tomorrow."

So saying she went to the door of the tank, and spoke; and now Tangle understood her perfectly.

"I want one of you," she said,—"the wisest."

Thereupon the fishes got together in the middle of the tank, with their heads forming a circle above the water, and their tails a larger circle beneath it. They were holding a council, in which their relative wisdom should be determined. At length one of them flew up into the lady's hand, looking lively and ready.

"You know where the rainbow stands?" she asked.

"Yes, Mother, quite well," answered the fish.

"Bring home a young man you will find there, who does not know where to go."

The fish was out of the door in a moment. Then the lady told Tangle it was time to go to bed; and, opening another door in the side of the cottage, showed her a little arbour, cool and green, with a bed of purple heath growing in it, upon which she threw a large wrapper made of the feathered skins of the wise fishes, shining gorgeous in the firelight. Tangle was soon lost in the strangest, loveliest dreams. And the beautiful lady was in every one of her dreams.

In the morning she awoke to the rustling of leaves over her head, and the sound of running water. But,

*Grandmother carried the winged creature to the door.*

to her surprise, she could find no door—nothing but the moss-grown wall of the cottage. So she crept through an opening in the arbour, and stood in the forest. Then she bathed in a stream that ran merrily through the trees, and felt happier; for having once been in her grandmother's pond, she must be clean and tidy ever after; and, having put on her green dress, felt like a lady.

She spent that day in the wood, listening to the birds and beasts and creeping things. She understood all that they said, though she could not repeat a word of it; and every kind had a different language, while there was a common though more limited under-standing between all the inhabitants of the forest. She saw nothing of the beautiful lady, but she felt that she was near her all the time; and she took care not to go out of sight of the cottage. It was round, like a snow-hut or a wigwam; and she could see neither door nor window in it. The fact was, it had no windows; and though it was full of doors, they all opened from the inside, and could not even be seen from the outside.

She was standing at the foot of a tree in the twi-light, listening to a quarrel between a mole and a squirrel, in which the mole told the squirrel that the tail was the best of him, and the squirrel called the mole Spade-fists, when, the darkness having deep-ened around her, she became aware of something shining in her face, and looking round, saw that the door of the cottage was open, and the red light of the fire flowing from it like a river through the darkness. She left Mole and Squirrel to settle matters as they might, and darted off to the cottage. Entering, she found the pot boiling on the fire, and the grand, lovely lady sitting on the other side of it.

"I've been watching you all day," said the lady. "You shall have something to eat by-and-by, but we must wait till our supper comes home."

She took Tangle on her knee, and began to sing to her—such songs as made her wish she could listen to them for ever. But at length in rushed the shining fish, and snuggled down in the pot. It was followed by a youth who had outgrown his worn garments. His face was ruddy with health, and in his hand he carried a little jewel, which sparkled in the firelight.

The first words the lady said were,—

"What is that in your hand, Mossy?"

Now Mossy was the name his companions had given him, because he had a favourite stone covered with moss, on which he used to sit whole days reading; and they said the moss had begun to grow upon him too.

Mossy held out his hand. The moment the lady saw that it was the golden key, she rose from her chair, kissed Mossy on the forehead, made him sit down on her seat, and stood before him like a servant. Mossy could not bear this, and rose at once. But the lady begged him, with tears in her beautiful eyes, to sit, and let her wait on him.

"But you are a great, splendid, beautiful lady," said Mossy.

"Yes, I am. But I work all day long—that is my pleasure; and you will have to leave me so soon!"

"How do you know that, if you please, madam?" asked Mossy.

"Because you have got the golden key."

"But I don't know what it is for. I can't find the keyhole. Will you tell me what to do?"

"You must look for the keyhole. That is your work. I cannot help you. I can only tell you that if you look for it you will find it."

"What kind of box will it open? What is there inside?"

"I do not know. I dream about it, but I know nothing."

15

"Must I go at once?"

"You may stop here to-night, and have some of my supper. But you must go in the morning. All I can do for you is to give you clothes. Here is a girl called Tangle, whom you must take with you."

"That *will* be nice," said Mossy.

"No, no!" said Tangle. "I don't want to leave you, please, Grandmother."

"You must go with him, Tangle. I am sorry to lose you, but it will be the best thing for you. Even the fishes, you see, have to go into the pot, and then out into the dark. If you fall in with the Old Man of the Sea, mind you ask him whether he has not got some more fishes ready for me. My tank is getting thin."

So saying, she took the fish from the pot, and put the lid on as before. They sat down and ate the fish, and then the winged creature rose from the pot, circled the roof, and settled on the lady's lap. She talked to it, carried it to the door, and threw it out into the dark. They heard the flap of its wings die away in the distance.

The lady then showed Mossy into just such another chamber as that of Tangle; and in the morning he found a suit of clothes laid beside him. He looked very handsome in them. But the wearer of Grandmother's clothes never thinks about how he or she looks, but thinks always how handsome other people are.

Tangle was very unwilling to go.

"Why should I leave you? I don't know the young man," she said to the lady.

"I am never allowed to keep my children long. You need not go with him except you please, but you must go some day; and I should like you to go with him, for he has the golden key. No girl need be afraid to go with a youth that has the golden key. You will take care of her, Mossy, will you not?"

"That I will," said Mossy.

And Tangle cast a glance at him, and thought she should like to go with him.

"And," said the lady, "if you should lose each other as you go through the—the—I never can remember the name of that country,—do not be afraid, but go on and on."

She kissed Tangle on the mouth and Mossy on the forehead, led them to the door, and waved her hand eastward. Mossy and Tangle took each other's hand and walked away into the depth of the forest. In his right hand Mossy held the golden key.

They wandered thus a long way, with endless amusement from the talk of the animals. They soon learned enough of their language to ask them necessary questions. The squirrels were always friendly, and gave them nuts out of their own hoards; but the bees were selfish and rude, justifying themselves on the ground that Tangle and Mossy were not subjects of their queen, and charity must begin at home, though indeed they had not one drone in their poorhouse at the time. Even the blinking moles would fetch them an earth-nut or a truffle now and then, talking as if their mouths, as well as their eyes and ears, were full of cotton wool, or their own velvety fur. By the time they got out of the forest they were very fond of each other, and Tangle was not in the least sorry that her grandmother had sent her away with Mossy.

At length the trees grew smaller, and stood farther apart, and the ground began to rise, and it got more and more steep, till the trees were all left behind, and the two were climbing a narrow path with rocks on each side. Suddenly they came upon a rude doorway, by which they entered a narrow gallery cut in the rock. It grew darker and darker, till it was pitch-dark, and they had to feel their way. At length the light began to return, and at last they came out upon a narrow path on the face of a lofty precipice. This path went winding down the rock to a wide plain, circular in shape, and surrounded on all sides by mountains. Those opposite to them were a great way off, and towered to an awful height, shooting up sharp, blue, ice-enamelled pinnacles. An utter silence reigned where they stood. Not even the sound of water reached them.

Looking down, they could not tell whether the valley below was a grassy plain or a great still lake. They had never seen any space look like it. The way to it was difficult and dangerous, but down the narrow path they went, and reached the bottom in safety. They found it composed of smooth, light-coloured sandstone, undulating in parts, but mostly level. It was no wonder to them now that they had not been able to tell what it was, for this surface was everywhere crowded with shadows. It was a sea of shadows. The mass was chiefly made up of the shadows of leaves innumerable, of all lovely and imaginative forms, waving to and fro, floating and quivering in the breath of a breeze whose motion was unfelt, whose sound was unheard. No forests clothed the mountainsides, no trees were anywhere to be seen, and yet the shadows of the leaves, branches, and stems of all various trees covered the valley as far as their eyes could reach. They soon spied the shadows of flowers mingled with those of the leaves, and now and then the shadow of a bird with open beak, and throat distended with song. At times would appear the forms of strange, graceful creatures, running up and down the shadow-boles and along the branches, to disappear in the wind-tossed foliage. As they walked they waded knee-deep in the lovely lake. For the shadows were not merely lying on the surface of the ground, but heaped up above it like substantial forms of darkness, as if they had been cast upon a thousand different planes of the air. Tangle and Mossy often lifted their heads and gazed upwards to descry whence the shadows came; but they could see nothing more than a bright mist spread above them, higher than the tops of the mountains, which stood clear against it. No forests, no leaves, no birds were visible.

After a while, they reached more open spaces, where the shadows were thinner; and came even to portions over which shadows only flitted, leaving them clear for such as might follow. Now a wonderful form, half bird-like half human, would float across on outspread sailing pinions. Anon an exquisite shadow group of gambolling children would be followed by the loveliest female form, and that again by the grand stride of a Titanic shape, each disappearing in the surrounding press of shadowy foliage. Sometimes a profile of unspeakable beauty or grandeur would appear for a moment and vanish. Sometimes they seemed lovers that passed linked arm in arm, sometimes father and son, sometimes brothers in loving contest, sometimes sisters entwined in gracefullest community of complex form. Sometimes wild horses would tear across, free, or bestrode by nobel shadows of ruling men. But some of the things which pleased them most they never knew how to describe.

About the middle of the plain they sat down to rest in the heart of a heap of shadows. After sitting for a while, each, looking up, saw the other in tears: they were each longing after the country whence the shadows fell.

"We *must* find the country from which the shadows come," said Mossy.

"We must, dear Mossy," responded Tangle. "What if your golden key should be the key to *it*?"

"Ah! that would be grand," returned Mossy. —"But

we must rest here for a little, and then we shall be able to cross the plain before night."

So he lay down on the ground, and about him on every side, and over his head, was the constant play of the wonderful shadows. He could look through them, and see the one behind the other, till they mixed in a mass of darkness. Tangle, too, lay admiring, and wondering, and longing after the country whence the shadows came. When they were rested they rose and pursued their journey.

How long they were in crossing this plain I cannot tell; but before night Mossy's hair was streaked with grey, and Tangle had got wrinkles on her forehead.

As evening drew on, the shadows fell deeper and rose higher. At length they reached a place where they rose above their heads, and made all dark around them. Then they took hold of each other's hand, and walked on in silence and in some dismay. They felt the gathering darkness, and something strangely solemn besides, and the beauty of the shadows ceased to delight them. All at once Tangle found that she had not a hold of Mossy's hand, though when she lost it she could not tell.

"Mossy, Mossy!" she cried aloud in terror.

But no Mossy replied.

A moment after, the shadows sank to her feet, and down under her feet, and the mountains rose before her. She turned towards the gloomy region she had left, and called once more upon Mossy. There the gloom lay tossing and heaving, a dark, stormy, foamless sea of shadows, but no Mossy rose out of it, or came climbing up the hill on which she stood. She threw herself down and wept in despair.

Suddenly she remembered that the beautiful lady had told them, if they lost each other in a country of which she could not remember the name, they were not to be afraid, but go straight on.

"And besides," she said to herself, "Mossy has the golden key, and so no harm will come to him, I do believe."

She rose from the ground, and went on.

Before long she arrived at a precipice, in the face of which a stair was cut. When she ascended half-way, the stair ceased, and the path led straight into the mountain. She was afraid to enter, and turning again towards the stair, grew giddy at the sight of the depth beneath her, and was forced to throw herself down in the mouth of the cave.

When she opened her eyes, she saw a beautiful little creature with wings standing beside her, waiting.

"I know you," said Tangle. "You are my fish."

"Yes. But I am a fish no longer. I am an aëranth now."

"What is that?" asked Tangle.

"What you see I am," answered the shape. "And I am come to lead you through the mountain."

"Oh! thank you, dear fish—aëranth, I mean," returned Tangle, rising.

Thereupon the aëranth took to his wings, and flew on through the long, narrow passage, reminding Tangle very much of the way he had swum on before when he was a fish. And the moment his white wings moved, they began to throw off a continuous shower of sparks of all colours, which lighted up the passage before them.—All at once he vanished, and Tangle heard a low, sweet sound, quite different from the rush and crackle of his wings. Before her was an open arch, and through it came light, mixed with the sound of sea-waves.

She hurried out, and fell, tired and happy, upon the yellow sand of the shore. There she lay, half asleep with weariness and rest, listening to the low plash and retreat of the tiny waves, which seemed ever enticing the land to leave off being land, and become sea. And as she lay, her eyes were fixed upon the foot of a great rainbow standing far away against the sky on the other side of the sea. At length she fell fast asleep.

When she awoke, she saw an old man with long white hair down to his shoulders, leaning upon a stick covered with green buds, and so bending over her.

"What do you want here, beautiful woman?" he said.

"Am I beautiful? I am so glad!" answered Tangle, rising. "My grandmother is beautiful."

"Yes. But what do you want?" He repeated, kindly.

"I think I want you. Are not you the Old Man of the Sea?"

"I am."

"Then Grandmother says, have you any more fishes ready for her?"

"We will go and see, my dear," answered the Old Man, speaking yet more kindly than before. "And I can do something for you, can I not?"

"Yes—show me the way up to the country from which the shadows fall," said Tangle.

For there she hoped to find Mossy again.

"Ah! indeed, that would be worth doing," said the old man. "But I cannot, for I do not know the way myself. But I will send you to the Old Man of the Earth. Perhaps he can tell you. He is much older than I am."

Leaning on his staff, he conducted her along the shore to a steep rock, that looked like a petrified ship turned upside down. The door of it was the rudder of a great vessel, ages ago at the bottom of the sea. Immediately within the door was a stair in the rock, down which the Old Man went, and Tangle followed. At the bottom the Old Man had his house, and there he lived.

As soon as she entered it, Tangle heard a strange noise, unlike anything she had ever heard before. She soon found that it was the fishes talking. She tried to understand what they said; but their speech was so old-fashioned, and rude, and undefined, that she could not make much of it.

"I will go and see about those fishes for my daughter," said the Old Man of the Sea.

And moving a slide in the wall of his house, he first looked out, and then tapped upon a thick piece of crystal that filled the round opening. Tangle came up behind him, and peeping through the window into the heart of the great deep green ocean, saw the most curious creatures, some very ugly, all very odd, and with especially queer mouths, swimming about everywhere, above and below, but all coming towards the window in answer to the tap of the Old Man of the Sea. Only a few could get their mouths against the glass; but those who were floating miles away yet turned their heads towards it. The Old Man looked through the whole flock carefully for some minutes, and then turning to Tangle, said,—

"I am sorry I have not got one ready yet. I want more time than she does. But I will send some as soon as I can."

He then shut the slide.

Presently a great noise arose in the sea. The Old Man opened the slide again, and tapped on the glass, whereupon the fishes were all as still as asleep.

"They were only talking about you," he said. "And they do speak such nonsense!—To-morrow," he continued, "I must show you the way to the Old Man of the Earth. He lives a long way from here."

"Do let me go at once," said Tangle.

"No, that is not possible. You must come this way first."

He led her to a hole in the wall, which she had not

23

observed before. It was covered with the green leaves and white blossoms of a creeping plant.

"Only white-blossoming plants can grow under the sea," said the Old Man. "In there you will find a bath, in which you must lie till I call you."

Tangle went in, and found a smaller room or cave, in the further corner of which was a great basin hollowed out of rock, and half-full of the clearest seawater. Little streams were constantly running into it from cracks in the wall of the cavern. It was polished quite smooth inside, and had a carpet of yellow sand in the bottom of it. Large green leaves and white flowers of various plants crowded up and over it, draping and covering it almost entirely.

No sooner was she undressed and lying in the bath, than she began to feel as if the water were sinking into her, and she were receiving all the good of sleep without undergoing its forgetfulness. She felt the good coming all the time. And she grew happier and more hopeful than she had been since she lost Mossy. But she could not help thinking how very sad it was for a poor old man to live there all alone, and have to take care of a whole seaful of stupid and riotous fishes.

After about an hour, as she thought, she heard his voice calling her, and rose out of the bath. All the fatigue and aching of her long journey had vanished. She was as whole, and strong, and well as if she had slept for seven days.

Returning to the opening that led into the other part of the house, she started back with amazement, for through it she saw the form of a grand man, with a majestic and beautiful face, waiting for her.

"Come," he said; "I see you are ready."

She entered with reverence.

"Where is the Old Man of the Sea?" she asked, humbly.

"There is no one here but me," he answered, smiling. "Some people call me the Old Man of the Sea. Others have another name for me, and are terribly frightened when they meet me taking a walk by the shore. Therefore I avoid being seen by them, for they are so afraid, that they never see what I really am. You see me now.—But I must show you the way to the Old Man of the Earth."

He led her into the cave where the bath was, and there she saw, in the opposite corner, a second opening in the rock.

"Go down that stair, and it will bring you to him," said the Old Man of the Sea.

With humble thanks Tangle took her leave. She went down the winding-stair, till she began to fear there was no end to it. Still down and down it went, rough and broken, with springs of water bursting out of the rocks and running down the steps beside her. It was quite dark about her, and yet she could see. For after being in that bath, people's eyes always give out a light they can see by. There were no creeping things in the way. All was safe and pleasant, though so dark and damp and deep.

At last there was not one step more, and she found herself in a glimmering cave. On a stone in the middle of it sat a figure with its back towards her—the figure of an old man bent double with age. From behind she could see his white beard spread out on the rocky floor in front of him. He did not move as she entered, so she passed round that she might stand before him and speak to him.

The moment she looked in his face, she saw that he was a youth of marvellous beauty. He sat entranced with the delight of what he beheld in a mirror of something like silver, which lay on the floor at his feet, and which from behind she had taken for his white beard. He sat on, heedless of her presence, pale with the joy of his vision. She stood and watched him. At length, all trembling, she spoke. But her voice made no sound. Yet the youth lifted up his head. He showed no surprise, however, at seeing her—only smiled a welcome.

"Are you the Old Man of the Earth?" Tangle had said.

And the youth answered, and Tangle heard him, though not with her ears:—

"I am. What can I do for you?"

"Tell me the way to the country whence the shadows fall."

"Ah! that I do not know. I only dream about it myself. I see its shadows sometimes in my mirror: the way to it I do not know. But I think the Old Man of the Fire must know. He is much older than I am. He is the oldest man of all."

"Where does he live?"

"I will show you the way to his place. I never saw him myself."

So saying, the young man rose, and then stood for a while gazing at Tangle.

"I wish I could see that country too," he said. "But I must mind my work."

He led her to the side of the cave, and told her to lay her ear against the wall.

"What do you hear?" he asked.

"I hear," answered Tangle, "the sound of a great water running inside the rock."

"That river runs down to the dwelling of the oldest man of all—the Old Man of the Fire. I wish I could go to see him. But I must mind my work. That river is the only way to him."

Then the Old Man of the Earth stooped over the floor of the cave, raised a huge stone from it, and left it leaning. It disclosed a great hole that went plumb-down.

"That is the way," he said.

"But there are no stairs."

"You must throw yourself in. There is no other way."

She turned and looked him full in the face—stood so for a whole minute, as she thought: it was a whole year—then threw herself headlong into the hole.

When she came to herself, she found herself gliding down fast and deep. Her head was under water, but that did not signify, for, when she thought about it, she could not remember that she had breathed once since her bath in the cave of the Old Man of the Sea. When she lifted up her head a sudden and fierce heat struck her, and she sank it again instantly, and went sweeping on.

Gradually the stream grew shallower. At length she could hardly keep her head under. Then the water could carry her no farther. She rose from the channel, and went step for step down the burning descent. The water ceased altogether. The heat was terrible. She felt scorched to the bone, but it did not touch her strength. It grew hotter and hotter. She said, "I can bear it no longer." Yet she went on.

At the long last, the stair ended at a rude archway in an all but glowing rock. Through this archway Tangle fell exhausted into a cool mossy cave. The floor and walls were covered with moss—green, soft, and damp. A little stream spouted from a rent in the rock and fell into a basin of moss. She plunged her face into it and drank. Then she lifted her head and looked around. Then she rose and looked again. She saw no one in the cave. But the moment she stood upright she had a marvellous sense that she was in the secret of the earth and all its ways. Everything she had seen, or learned from books; all that her grandmother had said or sung to her; all the talk of the beasts, birds, and fishes; all that happened to her on her journey with Mossy, and since then in the heart of the earth with the Old man and the Older man—all was plain: she understood it all, and saw that every-thing meant the same thing, though she could not have put it into words again.

The next moment she descried, in a corner of the cave, a little naked child, sitting on the moss. He was playing with balls of various colours and sizes, which he disposed in strange figures upon the floor beside him. And now Tangle felt that there was something in her knowledge which was not in her understand-ing. For she knew there must be an infinite meaning in the change and sequence and individual forms of the figures into which the child arranged the balls, as well as in the varied harmonies of their colours, but what it all meant she could not tell.* He went on busily, tirelessly, playing his solitary game, without looking up, or seeming to know that there was a stranger in his deep-withdrawn cell. Diligently as a lace-maker shifts her bobbins, he shifted and arranged his balls. Flashes of meaning would now pass from them to Tangle, and now again all would be not merely obscure, but utterly dark. She stood looking for a long time, for there was fascination in the sight; and the longer she looked the more an indescribable vague intelligence went on rousing itself in her mind. For seven years she had stood there watching the naked child with his coloured balls, and it seemed to her like seven hours, when all at once the shape the balls took, she know not why, reminded her of the Valley of Shadows, and she spoke:—

"Where is the Old Man of the Fire?" she said.

"Here I am," answered the child, rising and leaving his balls on the moss. "What can I do for you?"

There was such an awfulness of absolute repose

*I think I must be indebted to Novalis for these geometrical figures.

on the face of the child that Tangle stood dumb before him. He had no smile, but the love in his large gray eyes was deep as the centre. And with the repose there lay on his face a shimmer as of moonlight, which seemed as if any moment it might break into such a ravishing smile as would cause the beholder to weep himself to death. But the smile never came, and the moonlight lay there unbroken. For the heart of the child was too deep for any smile to reach from it to his face.

"Are you the oldest man of all?" Tangle at length, although filled with awe, ventured to ask.

"Yes, I am. I am very, very old. I am able to help you, I know. I can help everybody."

And the child drew near and looked up in her face so that she burst into tears.

"Can you tell me the way to the country the shadows fall from?" she sobbed.

"Yes. I know the way quite well. I go there myself sometimes. But you could not go my way; you are not old enough. I will show you how you can go."

"Do not send me out into the great heat again," prayed Tangle.

"I will not," answered the child.

And he reached up, and put his little cool hand on her heart.

"Now," he said, "you can go. The fire will not burn you. Come."

He led her from the cave, and following him through another archway, she found herself in a vast desert of sand and rock. The sky of it was of rock, lowering over them like solid thunderclouds; and the whole place was so hot that she saw, in bright rivulets, the yellow gold and white silver and red copper trickling molten from the rocks. But the heat never came near her.

When they had gone some distance, the child

turned up a great stone, and took something like an egg from under it. He next drew a long curved line in the sand with his finger, and laid the egg in it. He then spoke something Tangle could not understand. The egg broke, a small snake came out, and, lying in the line in the sand, grew and grew till he filled it. The moment he was thus full-grown, he began to glide away, undulating like a sea-wave.

"Follow that serpent," said the child. "He will lead you the right way."

Tangle followed the serpent. But she could not go far without looking back at the marvellous child. He stood alone in the midst of the glowing desert, beside a fountain of red flame that had burst forth at his feet, his naked whiteness glimmering a pale rosy red in the torrid fire. There he stood, looking after her, till, from the lengthening distance, she could see him no more. The serpent went straight on, turning neither to the right nor left.

Meantime Mossy had got out of the lake of shadows, and, following his mournful, lonely way, had reached the sea-shore. It was a dark, stormy evening. The sun had set. The wind was blowing from the sea. The waves had surrounded the rock within which lay the Old Man's house. A deep water rolled between it and the shore, upon which a majestic figure was walking alone.

Mossy went up to him and said,—

"Will you tell me where to find the Old Man of the Sea?"

"I am the Old Man of the Sea," the figure answered.

"I see a strong kingly man of middle age," returned Mossy.

Then the Old Man looked at him more intently, and said,—

"Your sight, young man, is better than that of most

30

who take this way. The night is stormy: come to my house and tell me what I can do for you."

Mossy followed him. The waves flew from before the footsteps of the Old Man of the Sea, and Mossy followed upon dry sand.

When they had reached the cave, they sat down and gazed at each other.

Now Mossy was an old man by this time. He looked much older than the Old Man of the Sea, and his feet were very weary.

After looking at him for a moment, the Old Man took him by the hand and led him into his inner cave. There he helped him to undress, and laid him in the bath. And he saw that one of his hands Mossy did not open.

"What have you in that hand?" he asked.

Mossy opened his hand, and there lay the golden key.

"Ah!" said the Old Man, "that accounts for your knowing me. And I know the way you have to go."

"I want to find the country whence the shadows fall," said Mossy.

"I dare say you do. So do I. But meantime, one thing is certain.—What is the key for, do you think?"

"For a keyhole somewhere. But I don't know why I keep it. I never could find the keyhole. And I have lived a good while, I believe," said Mossy, sadly. "I'm not sure that I'm not old. I know my feet ache."

"Do they?" said the Old Man, as if he really meant to ask the question: and Mossy, who was still lying in the bath, watched his feet for a moment before he replied.

"No, they do not," he answered. "Perhaps I am not old either."

"Get up and look at yourself in the water."

He rose and looked at himself in the water, and

there was not a gray hair on his head or a wrinkle on his skin.

"You have tasted of death now," said the Old Man. "Is it good?"

"It is good," said Mossy. "It is better than life."

"No," said the Old Man; "it is only more life.—Your feet will make no holes in the water now."

"What do you mean?"

"I will show you that presently."

They returned to the outer cave, and sat and talked together for a long time. At length the Old Man of the Sea rose, and said to Mossy,—

"Follow me."

He led him up the stair again, and opened another door. They stood on the level of the raging sea, looking towards the east. Across the waste of waters, against the bosom of a fierce black cloud, stood the foot of a rainbow, glowing in the dark.

"This indeed is my way," said Mossy, as soon as he saw the rainbow, and stepped out upon the sea. His feet made no holes in the water. He fought the wind, and clomb the waves, and went on towards the rainbow.

The storm died away. A lovely day and a lovelier night followed. A cool wind blew over the wide plain of the quiet ocean. And still Mossy journeyed eastward. But the rainbow had vanished with the storm.

Day after day he held on, and he thought he had no guide. He did not see how a shining fish under the waters directed his steps. He crossed the sea, and came to a great precipice of rock, up which he could discover but one path. Nor did this lead him farther than half-way up the rock, where it ended on a platform. Here he stood and pondered.—It could not be that the way stopped here, else what was the path for? It was a rough path, not very plain, yet certainly a path.—He examined the face of the rock.

It was smooth as glass. But as his eyes kept roving hopelessly over it, something glittered, and he caught sight of a row of small sapphires. They bordered a little hole in the rock.

"The keyhole!" he cried.

He tried the key. It fitted. It turned. A great clang and clash, as of iron bolts on huge brazen caldrons, echoed thunderously within. He drew out the key. The rock in front of him began to fall. He retreated from it as far as the breadth of the platform would allow. A great slab fell at his feet. In front was still the solid rock, with this one slab fallen forward out of it. But the moment he stepped upon it, a second fell, just short of the edge of the first, making the next step of a stair, which thus kept dropping itself before him as he ascended into the heart of the precipice. It led him into a hall fit for such an approach—irregular and rude in formation, but floor, sides, pillars, and vaulted roof, all one mass of shining stones of every colour that light can show. In the centre stood seven columns, ranged from red to violet. And on the pedestal of one of them sat a woman, motionless, with her face bowed upon her knees. Seven years had she sat there waiting. She lifted her head as Mossy drew near. It was Tangle. Her hair had grown to her feet, and was rippled like the windless sea on broad sands. Her face was beautiful, like her grandmother's, and as still and peaceful as that of the Old Man of the Fire. Her form was tall and noble. Yet Mossy knew her at once.

"How beautiful you are, Tangle!" he said, in delight and astonishment.

"Am I?" she returned. "Oh, I have waited for you so long! But you, you are like the Old Man of the Sea. No. You are like the Old Man of the Earth. No, no. You are like the oldest man of all. You are like them all. And yet you are my own old Mossy! How did you

come here? What did you do after I lost you? Did you find the keyhole? Have you got the key still?"

She had a hundred questions to ask him, and he a hundred more to ask her. They told each other all their adventures, and were as happy as man and woman could be. For they were younger and better, and stronger and wiser, than they had ever been before.

34

It began to grow dark. And they wanted more than ever to reach the country whence the shadows fall. So they looked about them for a way out of the cave. The door by which Mossy entered had closed again, and there was half a mile of rock between them and the sea. Neither could Tangle find the opening in the floor by which the serpent had led her thither. They searched till it grew so dark that they could see nothing, and gave it up.

After a while, however, the cave began to glimmer again. The light came from the moon, but it did not look like moonlight, for it gleamed through those seven pillars in the middle, and filled the place with all colours. And now Mossy saw that there was a pillar beside the red one, which he had not observed before. And it was of the same new colour that he had seen in the rainbow when he saw it first in the fairy forest. And on it he saw a sparkle of blue. It was the sapphires round the keyhole.

He took his key. It turned in the lock to the sounds of Aeolian music. A door opened upon slow hinges, and disclosed a winding stair within. The key vanished from his fingers. Tangle went up. Mossy followed. The door closed behind them. They climbed out of the earth; and, still climbing, rose above it. They were in the rainbow. Far abroad, over ocean and land, they could see through its transparent walls the earth beneath their feet. Stairs beside stairs wound up together, and beautiful beings of all ages climbed along with them.

They knew that they were going up to the country whence the shadows fall.

And by this time I think they must have got there.

35

# THE HISTORY OF PHOTOGEN AND NYCTERIS
## A Day and Night Mährchen

### I: WATHO

HERE was once a witch who desired to know everything. But the wiser a witch is, the harder she knocks her head against the wall when she comes to it. Her name was Watho, and she had a wolf in her mind. She cared for nothing in itself—only for knowing it. She was not naturally cruel but the wolf had made her cruel.

She was tall and graceful, with a white skin, red hair, and black eyes, which had a red fire in them. She was straight and strong, but now and then would fall bent together, shudder, and sit for a moment with her head turned over her shoulder, as if the wolf had got out of her mind on to her back.

### II: AURORA

THIS witch got two ladies to visit her. One of them belonged to the court, and her husband had been sent on a far and difficult embassy. The other was a young widow whose husband had lately

Reprinted from *Graphic*, Christmas Number (1879).

died, and who had since lost her sight. Watho lodged them in different parts of her castle, and they did not know of each other's existence.

The castle stood on the side of a hill sloping gently down into a narrow valley, in which was a river, with a pebbly channel and a continual song. The garden went down to the bank of the river, enclosed by high walls, which crossed the river and there stopped. Each wall had a double row of battlements, and between the rows was a narrow walk.

In the topmost story of the castle the Lady Aurora occupied a spacious apartment of several large rooms looking southward. The windows projected oriel-wise over the garden below, and there was a splendid view from them both up and down and across the river. The opposite side of the valley was steep, but not very high. Far away snowpeaks were visible. These rooms Aurora seldom left, but their airy spaces, the brilliant landscape and sky, the plentiful sunlight, the musical instruments, books, pictures, curiosities, with the company of Watho, who made herself charming, precluded all dulness. She had venison and feathered game to eat, milk and pale sunny sparkling wine to drink.

She had hair of the yellow gold, waved and rippled; her skin was fair, not white like Watho's, and her eyes were of the blue of the heavens when bluest; her features were delicate but strong, her mouth large and finely curved, and haunted with smiles.

## III: VESPER

BEHIND the castle the hill rose abruptly; the north-eastern tower, indeed, was in contact with the rock, and communicated with the interior of it. For in the rock was a series of chambers, known only to Watho and the one servant whom she trusted, called Falca. Some former owner had constructed these chambers after the tomb of an Egyptian king, and probably with the same design, for in the centre of one of them stood what could only be a sarcophagus, but that and others were walled off. The sides and roofs of them were carved in low relief, and curiously painted. Here the witch lodged the blind lady, whose name was Vesper. Her eyes were black, with long black lashes; her skin had a look of darkened silver, but was of purest tint and grain; her hair was black and fine and straight-flowing; her features were exquisitely formed, and if less beautiful yet more lovely from sadness; she always looked as if she wanted to lie down and not rise again. She did not know she was lodged in a tomb, though now and then she wondered she never touched a window. There were many couches, covered with richest silk, and soft as her own cheek, for her to lie upon; and the carpets were so thick, she might have cast herself down anywhere—as befitted a tomb. The place was dry and warm, and cunningly pierced for air, so that it was always fresh, and lacked only sunlight. There the witch fed her upon milk, and wine dark as a carbuncle, and pomegranates, and purple grapes, and birds that dwell in marshy places; and she played to her mournful tunes, and caused wailful violins to attend her, and told her sad tales, thus holding her ever in an atmosphere of sweet sorrow.

## IV: PHOTOGEN

ATHO at length had her desire, for witches often get what they want: a splendid boy was born to the fair Aurora. Just as the sun rose, he opened his eyes. Watho carried him immediately to a distant part of the castle, and persuaded the mother that he never cried but once, dying the moment he was born. Overcome with grief, Aurora left the castle as soon as she was able, and Watho never invited her again.

And now the witch's care was, that the child should not know darkness. Persistently she trained him until at last he never slept during the day, and never woke during the night. She never let him see anything black, and even kept all dull colours out of his way. Never, if she could help it, would she let a shadow fall upon him, watching against shadows as if they had been live things that would hurt him. All day he basked in the full splendour of the sun, in the same large rooms his mother had occupied. Watho used him to the sun, until he could bear more of it than any dark-blooded African. In the hottest of every day, she stript him and laid him in it, that he might ripen like a peach; and the boy rejoiced in it, and would resist being dressed again. She brought all her knowledge to bear on making his muscles strong and elastic and swiftly responsive—that his soul, she said laughing, might sit in every fibre, be all in every part, and awake the moment of call. His hair was of the red gold, but his eyes grew darker as he grew, until they were as black as Vesper's. He was the merriest of creatures, always laughing, always loving, for a moment raging, then laughing afresh. Watho called him Photogen.

## V: NYCTERIS

FIVE or six months after the birth of Photogen, the dark lady also gave birth to a baby: in the windowless tomb of a blind mother, in the dead of night, under the feeble rays of a lamp in an alabaster globe, a girl came into the darkness with a wail. And just as she was born for the first time, Vesper was born for the second, and passed into a world as unknown to her as this was to her child—who would have to be born yet again before she could see her mother.

Watho called her Nycteris, and she grew as like Vesper as possible—in all but one particular. She had the same dark skin, dark eyelashes and brows, dark hair, and gentle sad look; but she had just the eyes of Aurora, the mother of Photogen, and if they grew darker as she grew older, it was only a darker blue. Watho, with the help of Falca, took the greatest possible care of her—in every way consistent with her plans, that is,—the main point in which was that she should never see any light but what came from the lamp. Hence her optic nerves, and indeed her whole apparatus for seeing, grew both larger and more sensitive; her eyes, indeed, stopped short only of being too large. Under her dark hair and forehead and eyebrows, they looked like two breaks in a cloudy night-sky, through which peeped the heaven where the stars and no clouds live. She was a sadly dainty little creature. No one in the world except those two was aware of the being of the little bat. Watho trained her to sleep during the day, and wake during the night. She taught her music, in which she was herself proficient, and taught her scarcely anything else.

## VI: HOW PHOTOGEN GREW

THE hollow in which the castle of Watho lay, was a cleft in a plain rather than a valley among hills, for at the top of its steep sides, both north and south, was a table-land, large and wide. It was covered with rich grass and flowers, with here and there a wood, the outlying colony of a great forest. These grassy plains were the finest hunting grounds in the world. Great herds of small, but fierce cattle, with humps and shaggy manes, roved about them, also antelopes and gnus, and the tiny roedeer, while the woods were

swarming with wild creatures. The tables of the castle were mainly supplied from them. The chief of
Watho's huntsmen was a fine fellow, and when Photogen began to outgrow the training she could give
him, she handed him over to Fargu. He with a will
set about teaching him all he knew. He got him pony
after pony, larger and larger as he grew, every one
less manageable than that which had preceded it, and
advanced him from pony to horse, and from horse to
horse, until he was equal to anything in that kind
which the country produced. In similar fashion he
trained him to the use of bow and arrow, substituting
every three months a stronger bow and longer arrows; and soon he became, even on horseback, a
wonderful archer. He was but fourteen when he killed
his first bull, causing jubilation among the huntsmen, and, indeed, through all the castle, for there too
he was the favourite. Every day, almost as soon as
the sun was up, he went out hunting, and would in
general be out nearly the whole of the day. But Watho
had laid upon Fargu just one commandment, namely,
that Photogen should on no account, whatever the
plea, be out until sundown, or so near it as to wake
in him the desire of seeing what was going to happen;
and this commandment Fargu was anxiously careful
not to break; for, although he would not have trem-
bled had a whole herd of bulls come down upon him,
charging at full speed across the level, and not an
arrow left in his quiver, he was more than afraid of
his mistress. When she looked at him in a certain
way, he felt, he said, as if his heart turned to ashes
in his breast, and what ran in his veins was no longer
blood, but milk and water. So that, ere long, as Photogen grew older, Fargu began to tremble, for he found
it steadily growing harder to restrain him. So full of
life was he, as Fargu said to his mistress, much to
her content, that he was more like a live thunderbolt

than a human being. He did not know what fear was, and that not because he did not know danger; for he had had a severe laceration from the razor-like tusk of a boar—whose spine, however, he had severed with one blow of his hunting-knife, before Fargu could reach him with defence. When he would spur his horse into the midst of a herd of bulls, carrying only his bow and his short sword, or shoot an arrow into a herd, and go after it as if to reclaim it for a runaway shaft, arriving in time to follow it with a spear-thrust before the wounded animal knew which way to charge, Fargu thought with terror how it would be when he came to know the temptation of the huddle-spot leopards, and the knife-clawed lynxes, with which the forest was haunted. For the boy had been so steeped in the sun, from childhood so saturated with his influence, that he looked upon every danger from a sovereign height of courage. When, therefore, he was approaching his sixteenth year, Fargu ventured to beg of Watho that she would lay her commands upon the youth himself, and release him from responsibility for him. One might as soon hold a tawny-maned lion as Photogen, he said. Watho called the youth, and in the presence of Fargu laid her command upon him never to be out when the rim of the sun should touch the horizon, accompanying the prohibition with hints of consequences, none the less awful that they were obscure. Photogen listened respectfully, but, knowing neither the taste of fear nor the temptation of the night, her words were but sounds to him.

## VII: HOW NYCTERIS GREW

THE little education she intended Nycteris to have, Watho gave her by word of mouth. Not meaning she should have light enough to read by, to leave other reasons unmentioned, she never put a book in her hands. Nycteris, however, saw so much better than Watho imagined, that the light she gave her was quite sufficient, and she managed to coax Falca into teaching her the letters, after which she taught herself to read, and Falca now and then brought her a child's book. But her chief pleasure was in her instrument. Her very fingers loved it, and would wander about over its keys like feeding sheep. She was not unhappy. She knew nothing of the world except the tomb in which she dwelt, and had some pleasure in everything she did. But she desired, nevertheless, something more or different. She did not know what it was, and the nearest she could come to expressing it to herself was—that she wanted more room. Watho and Falca would go from her beyond the shine of the lamp, and come again; therefore surely there must be more room somewhere. As often as she was left alone, she would fall to poring over the coloured bas-reliefs on the walls. These were intended to represent various of the powers of Nature under allegorical similitudes, and as nothing can be made that does not belong to the general scheme, she could not fail at least to imagine a flicker of relationship between some of them, and thus a shadow of the reality of things found its way to her.

There was one thing, however, which moved and taught her more than all the rest—the lamp, namely, that hung from the ceiling, which she always saw alight, though she never saw the flame, only the slight condensation towards the centre of the alabaster globe. And besides the operation of the light itself after its kind, the indefiniteness of the globe, and the softness of the light, giving her the feeling as if her eyes could go in and into its whiteness, were somehow also associated with the idea of space and room. She would sit for an hour together gazing up at the lamp, and her heart would swell as she gazed. She would wonder what had hurt her, when she found her face wet with tears, and then would wonder how she could have been hurt without knowing it. She never looked thus at the lamp except when she was alone.

## VIII: THE LAMP

WATHO having given orders, took it for granted they were obeyed, and that Falca was all night long with Nycteris, whose day it was. But Falca could not get into the habit of sleeping through the day, and would often leave her alone half the night. Then it seemed to Nycteris that the white lamp was watching over her. As it was never permitted to go out—except while she was awake at least—Nycteris, except by shutting her eyes, knew less about darkness than she did about light. Also, the lamp being fixed high overhead, and in the centre of everything, she did not know much about shadows either. The few there were fell almost entirely on the floor, or kept like mice about the foot of the walls.

Once, when she was thus alone, there came the noise of a far-off rumbling: she had never before heard a sound of which she did not know the origin, and here therefore was a new sign of something beyond these chambers. Then came a trembling, then a shaking; the lamp dropped from the ceiling to the floor with a great crash, and she felt as if both her eyes were hard shut and both her hands over them. She concluded that it was the darkness that had made the rumbling and the shaking, and rushing into the room, had thrown down the lamp. She sat trembling. The noise and the shaking ceased, but the light did not return. The darkness had eaten it up!

Her lamp gone, the desire at once awoke to get out of her prison. She scarcely knew what *out* meant; out of one room into another, where there was not even a dividing door, only an open arch, was all she knew of the world. But suddenly she remembered that she had heard Falca speak of the lamp *going out:* this must be what she had meant? And if the lamp had gone out, where had it gone? Surely where Falca went, and like her it would come again. But she could not wait. The desire to go out grew irresistible. She must follow her beautiful lamp! She must find it! She must see what it was about!

Now there was a curtain covering a recess in the wall, where some of her toys and gymnastic things were kept; and from behind that curtain Watho and Falca always appeared, and behind it they vanished. How they came out of solid wall, she had not an idea, all up to the wall was open space, and all beyond it seemed wall; but clearly the first and only thing she could do, was to feel her way behind the curtain. It was so dark that a cat could not have caught the largest of mice. Nycteris could see better than any cat, but now her great eyes were not of the smallest use to her. As she went she trod upon a piece of the broken lamp. She had never worn shoes or stockings, and the fragment, though, being of soft alabaster, it did not cut, yet hurt her foot. She did not know what it was, but as it had not been there before the darkness came, she suspected that it had to do with the lamp. She kneeled therefore, and searched with her hands, and bringing two large pieces together, recognized the shape of the lamp. Therewith it flashed upon her that the lamp was dead, that this brokenness was the death of which she had read without understanding, that the darkness had killed the lamp. What then could Falca have meant when she spoke of the lamp *going out?* There was the lamp—dead, indeed, and so changed that she would never have taken it for a lamp but for the shape! No, it was not the lamp any more now it was dead, for all that made it a lamp was gone, namely, the bright shining of it. Then it must be the shine, the light, that had gone out! That must be what Falca meant—and it must be somewhere in the other place in the wall. She started afresh after it, and groped her way to the curtain.

Now she had never in her life tried to get out, and did not know how; but instinctively she began to move her hands about over one of the walls behind the curtain, half expecting them to go into it, as she supposed Watho and Falca did. But the wall repelled her with inexorable hardness, and she turned to the one opposite. In so doing, she set her foot upon an ivory die, and as it met sharply the same spot the broken alabaster had already hurt, she fell forward with her outstretched hands against the wall. Something gave way, and she tumbled out of the cavern.

## IX: OUT

BUT alas! *out* was very much like *in*, for the same enemy, the darkness, was here also. The next moment, however, came a great gladness—a firefly, which had wandered in from the garden. She saw the tiny spark in the distance. With slow pulsing ebb and throb of light, it came pushing itself through the air, drawing nearer and nearer, with that motion which more resembles swimming than flying, and the light seemed the source of its own motion.

"My lamp! my lamp!" cried Nycteris. "It is the shiningness of my lamp, which the cruel darkness drove out. My good lamp has been waiting for me here all the time! It knew I would come after it, and waited to take me with it."

She followed the firefly, which, like herself, was seeking the way out. If it did not know the way, it was yet light; and, because all light is one, any light may serve to guide to more light. If she was mistaken in thinking it the spirit of her lamp, it was of the same spirit as her lamp—and had wings. The gold-green jet-boat, driven by light, went throbbing before her through a long, narrow passage. Suddenly it rose higher, and the same moment Nycteris fell upon an ascending stair. She had never seen a stair before, and found going-up a curious sensation. Just as she reached what seemed the top, the firefly ceased to shine, and so disappeared. She was in utter darkness once more. But when we are following the light, even its extinction is a guide. If the firefly had gone on shining, Nycteris would have seen the stair turn, and would have gone up to Watho's bedroom, whereas now, feeling straight before her, she came to a latched door, which after a good deal of trying she managed to open—and stood in a maze of wondering perplexity, awe, and delight. What was it? Was it outside of her, or something taking place in her head? Before her was a very long and very narrow passage, broken up she could not tell how, and spreading out above and on all sides to an infinite height and breadth and distance—as if space itself were growing out of a trough. It was brighter than her rooms had ever been—brighter than if six alabaster lamps had been burning in them. There was a quantity of strange streaking and mottling about it, very different from the shapes on her walls. She was in a dream of pleasant perplexity, of delightful bewilderment. She could not tell whether she was upon her feet or drifting about like the firefly, driven by the pulses of an inward bliss. But she knew little as yet of her inheritance. Unconsciously she took one step forward from the threshold, and the girl who had been from her very birth a troglodyte,* stood in the ravishing glory

*A cave dweller.

of a southern night, lit by a perfect moon—not the moon of our northern clime, but a moon like silver glowing in a furnace—a moon one could see to be a globe—not far off, a mere flat disc on the face of the blue, but hanging down half-way, and looking as if one could see all round it by a mere bending of the neck.

"It is my lamp!" she said, and stood dumb with parted lips. She looked and felt as if she had been standing there in silent ecstasy from the beginning.

"No, it is not my lamp," she said after a while; "it is the mother of all the lamps."

And with that she fell on her knees, and spread out her hands to the moon. She could not in the least have told what was in her mind, but the action was in reality just a begging of the moon to be what she was—that precise incredible splendour hung in the far-off roof, that very glory essential to the being of poor girls born and bred in caverns. It was a resurrection—nay, a birth itself, to Nycteris. What the vast blue sky, studded with tiny sparks like the heads of diamond nails, could be; what the moon, looking so absolutely content with light—why, she knew less about them than you and I! but the greatest of astronomers might envy the rapture of such a first impression at the age of sixteen. Immeasurably imperfect it was, but false the impression could not be, for she saw with the eyes made for seeing, and saw indeed what many men are too wise to see.

As she knelt, something softly flapped her, embraced her, stroked her, fondled her. She rose to her feet, but saw nothing, did not know what it was. It was likest a woman's breath. For she knew nothing of the air even, had never breathed the still, newborn freshness of the world. Her breath had come to her only through long passages and spirals in the rock. Still less did she know of the air alive with motion—of that thrice blessed thing, the wind of a summer

*The wind of the summer night was like a spiritual wine,*
*filling Nycteris' whole being with an intoxication of purest joy.*

night. It was like a spiritual wine, filling her whole being with an intoxication of purest joy. To breathe was a perfect existence. It seemed to her the light itself she drew into her lungs. Possessed by the power of the gorgeous night, she seemed at one and the same moment annihilated and glorified.

She was in the open passage or gallery that ran round the top of the garden walls, between the cleft battlements, but she did not once look down to see what lay beneath. Her soul was drawn to the vault above her, with its lamp and its endless room. At last she burst into tears, and her heart was relieved, as the night itself is relieved by its lightning and rain.

And now she grew thoughtful. She must hoard this splendour! What a little ignorance her gaolers had made of her! Life was a mighty bliss, and they had scraped hers to the bare bone! They must not know that she knew. She must hide her knowledge— hide it even from her own eyes, keeping it close in her bosom, content to know that she had it, even when she could not brood on its presence, feasting her eyes with its glory. She turned from the vision, therefore, with a sigh of utter bliss, and with soft quiet steps and groping hands, stole back into the darkness of the rock. What was darkness or the laziness of Time's feet to one who had seen what she had that night seen? She was lifted above all weariness—above all wrong.

When Falca entered, she uttered a cry of terror. But Nycteris called to her not to be afraid, and told her how there had come a rumbling and a shaking, and the lamp had fallen. Then Falca went and told her mistress, and within an hour a new globe hung in the place of the old one. Nycteris thought it did not look so bright and clear as the former, but she made no lamentation over the change; she was far too rich to heed it. For now, prisoner as she knew herself, her heart was full of glory and gladness; at times she had to hold herself from jumping up, and going dancing and singing about the room. When she slept, instead of dull dreams, she had splendid visions. There were times, it is true, when she became restless, and impatient to look upon her riches, but, then she would reason with herself, saying, "What does it matter if I sit here for ages with my poor pale lamp, when out there a lamp is burning at which ten thousand little lamps are glowing with wonder?"

She never doubted she had looked upon the day and the sun, of which she had read; and always when she read of the day and the sun, she had the night and the moon in her mind; and when she read of the night and the moon, she thought only of the cave and the lamp that hung there.

## X: THE GREAT LAMP

IT was some time before she had a second opportunity of going out, for Falca, since the fall of the lamp, had been a little more careful, and seldom left her for long. But one night, having a little headache, Nycteris lay down upon her bed, and was lying with her eyes closed, when she heard Falca come to her, and felt she was bending over her. Disinclined to talk, she did not open her eyes, and lay quite still. Satisfied that she was asleep, Falca left her, moving so softly that her very caution made Nycteris open her eyes and look after her—just in time to see her vanish—through a picture, as it seemed, that hung on the wall a long way from the usual place of issue. She jumped up, her headache forgotten, and ran in the opposite direction; got out, groped her way to the stair, climbed, and reached the top of the wall.—Alas! the great room was not so light as the little one she

had left. Why?—Sorrow of sorrows! the great lamp
was gone! Had its globe fallen? and its lovely light
gone out upon great wings, a resplendent firefly, oar-
ing itself through a yet grander and lovelier room?
She looked down to see if it lay anywhere broken to
pieces on the carpet below; but she could not even
see the carpet. But surely nothing very dreadful could
have happened—no rumbling or shaking, for there
were all the little lamps shining brighter than before,
not one of them looking as if any unusual matter had
befallen. What if each of those little lamps was growing into a big lamp, and after being a big lamp for a
while, had to go out and grow a bigger lamp still—
out there, beyond this *out*?—Ah! here was the living
thing that would not be seen, come to her again—
bigger to-night! with such loving kisses, and such
liquid strokings of her cheeks and forehead, gently
tossing her hair, and delicately toying with it! But it
ceased, and all was still. Had it gone out? What would
happen next? Perhaps the little lamps had not to grow
great lamps, but to fall one by one and go out first?—
With that, came from below a sweet scent, then another, and another. Ah, how delicious! Perhaps they
were all coming to her only on their way out after the
great lamp!—Then came the music of the river, which
she had been too absorbed in the sky to note the first
time. What was it? Alas! alas! another sweet living
thing on its way out. They were all marching slowly
out in long lovely file, one after the other, each taking
its leave of her as it passed! It must be so: here were
more and more sweet sounds, following and fading!
The whole of the *Out* was going out again; it was all
going after the great lovely lamp! She would be left
the only creature in the solitary day! Was there nobody to hang up a new lamp for the old one, and keep
the creatures from going?—She crept back to her rock
very sad. She tried to comfort herself by saying that

anyhow there would be room out there; but as she said it she shuddered at the thought of *empty* room.

When next she succeeded in getting out, a half-moon hung in the east: a new lamp had come, she thought, and all would be well.

It would be endless to describe the phases of feeling through which Nycteris passed, more numerous and delicate than those of a thousand changing moons. A fresh bliss bloomed in her soul with every varying aspect of infinite nature. Ere long she began to suspect that the new moon was the old moon, gone out and come in again like herself; also that, unlike herself, it wasted and grew again; that it was indeed a live thing, subject like herself to caverns, and keepers, and solitudes, escaping and shining when it could. Was it a prison like hers it was shut in? and did it grow dark when the lamp left it? Where could be the way into it?—With that first she began to look below, as well as above and around her; and then first noted the tops of the trees between her and the floor. There were palms with their red-fingered hands full of fruit; eucalyptus trees crowded with little boxes of powder-puffs; oleanders with their half-caste roses; and orange trees with their clouds of young silver stars, and their aged balls of gold. Her eyes could see colours invisible to ours in the moonlight, and all these she could distinguish well, though at first she took them for the shapes and colours of the carpet of the great room. She longed to get down among them, now she saw they were real creatures, but she did not know how. She went along the whole length of the wall to the end that crossed the river, but found no way of going down. Above the river she stopped to gaze with awe upon the rushing water. She knew nothing of water but from what she drank and what she bathed in; and, as the moon shone on the dark, swift stream, singing lustily as it flowed, she did not doubt the river was alive, a swift rushing serpent of life, going—out?—whither? And then she wondered if what was brought into her rooms had been killed that she might drink it, and have her bath in it.

Once when she stepped out upon the wall, it was into the midst of a fierce wind. The trees were all roaring. Great clouds were rushing along the skies, and tumbling over the little lamps: the great lamp had not come yet. All was in tumult. The wind seized her garments and hair, and shook them as if it would tear them from her. What could she have done to make the gentle creature so angry? Or was this another creature altogether—of the same kind, but hugely bigger, and of a very different temper and behaviour? But the whole place was angry! Or was it that the creatures dwelling in it, the wind, and the trees, and the clouds, and the river, had all quarrelled, each with all the rest? Would the whole come to confusion and disorder? But, as she gazed wondering and dis- quieted, the moon, larger than ever she had seen her, came lifting herself above the horizon to look, broad and red as if she, too, were swollen with anger that she had been roused from her rest by their noise, and compelled to hurry up to see what her children were about, thus rioting in her absence, lest they should rack the whole frame of things. And as she rose, the loud wind grew quieter and scolded less fiercely, the trees grew stiller and moaned with a lower complaint, and the clouds hunted and hurled themselves less wildly across the sky. And as if she were pleased that her children obeyed her very presence, the moon grew smaller as she ascended the heavenly stair; her puffed cheeks sank, her complexion grew clearer, and a sweet smile spread over her countenance, as peacefully she rose and rose. But there was treason and rebellion in her court; for, ere she reached the top of her great stairs, the clouds had assembled, forgetting their late wars, and very still they were as they laid their heads together and conspired. Then combining, and lying silently in wait until she came near, they threw themselves upon her, and swallowed her up. Down from the roof came spots of wet, faster and faster, and they wetted the cheeks of Nycteris; and what could they be but the tears of the moon, crying because her children were smothering her? Nycteris wept too, and not knowing what to think, stole back in dismay to her room.

The next time, she came out in fear and trembling. There was the moon still! away in the west—poor, indeed, and old, and looking dreadfully worn, as if all the wild beasts in the sky had been gnawing at her— but there she was, alive still, and able to shine!

## XI: THE SUNSET

KNOWING nothing of darkness, or stars, or moon, Photogen spent his days in hunting. On a great white horse he swept over the grassy plains, glorying in the sun, fighting the wind, and killing the buffaloes.

One morning, when he happened to be on the ground a little earlier than usual, and before his attendants, he caught sight of an animal unknown to him, stealing from a hollow into which the sunrays had not yet reached. Like a swift shadow it sped over the grass, slinking southward to the forest. He gave chase, noted the body of a buffalo it had half eaten, and pursued it the harder. But with great leaps and bounds the creature shot farther and farther ahead of him, and vanished. Turning therefore defeated, he met Fargu, who had been following him as fast as his horse could carry him.

"What animal was that, Fargu?" he asked. "How he did run!"

Fargu answered he might be a leopard, but he rather thought from his pace and look that he was a young lion.

"What a coward he must be!" said Photogen.

"Don't be too sure of that," rejoined Fargu. "He is one of the creatures the sun makes uncomfortable. As soon as the sun is down, he will be brave enough.

He had scarcely said it, when he repented; nor did he regret it the less when he found that Photogen made no reply. But alas! said was said.

"Then," said Photogen to himself, "that contemptible beast is one of the terrors of sundown, of which Madam Watho spoke!"

He hunted all day, but not with his usual spirit. He did not ride so hard, and did not kill one buffalo. Fargu to his dismay observed also that he took every pretext for moving farther south, nearer to the forest. But all at once, the sun now sinking in the west, he seemed to change his mind, for he turned his horse's head, and rode home so fast that the rest could not keep him in sight. When they arrived, they found his horse in the stable, and concluded that he had gone into the castle. But he had in truth set out again by the back of it. Crossing the river a good way up the valley, he reascended to the ground they had left, and just before sunset reached the skirts of the forest.

The level orb shone straight in between the bare stems, and saying to himself he could not fail to find the beast, he rushed into the wood. But even as he entered, he turned, and looked to the west. The rim of the red was touching the horizon, all jagged with broken hills. "Now," said Photogen, "we shall see"; but he said it in the face of a darkness he had not proved. The moment the sun began to sink among the spikes and saw-edges, with a kind of sudden flap at his heart a fear inexplicable laid hold of the youth; and as he had never felt anything of the kind before,

*On a great white horse Photogen swept over the grassy plains,*
*glorying in the sun and fighting the wind.*

57

the very fear itself terrified him. As the sun sank, it rose like the shadow of the world, and grew deeper and darker. He could not even think what it might be, so utterly did it enfeeble him. When the last flaming scimitar-edge of the sun went out like a lamp, his horror seemed to blossom into very madness. Like the closing lids of an eye—for there was no twilight, and this night no moon—the terror and the darkness rushed together, and he knew them for one. He was no longer the man he had known, or rather thought himself. The courage he had had was in no sense his own—he had only had courage, not been courageous; it had left him, and he could scarcely stand—certainly not stand straight, for not one of his joints could he make stiff or keep from trembling. He was but a spark of the sun, in himself nothing.

The beast was behind him—stealing upon him! He turned. All was dark in the wood, but to his fancy the darkness here and there broke into pairs of green eyes, and he had not the power even to raise his bow-hand from his side. In the strength of despair he strove to rouse courage enough—not to fight—that he did not even desire—but to run. Courage to flee home was all he could ever imagine, and it would not come. But what he had not, was ignominiously given him. A cry in the wood, half a screech, half a growl, sent him running like a boar-wounded cur. It was not even himself that ran, it was the fear that had come alive in his legs: he did not know that they moved. But as he ran he grew able to run—gained courage at least to be a coward. The stars gave a little light. Over the grass he sped, and nothing followed him. "How fallen, how changed," from the youth who had climbed the hill as the sun went down! A mere contempt to himself, the self that contemned was a coward with the self it contemned! There lay the shapeless black of a buffalo, humped upon the grass; he made a wide circuit, and swept on like a shadow driven in the wind. For the wind had arisen, and added to his terror: it blew from behind him. He reached the brow of the valley, and shot down the steep descent like a falling star. Instantly the whole upper country behind him arose and pursued him! The wind came howling after him, filled with screams, shrieks, yells, roars, laughter, and chattering, as if all the animals of the forest were careering with it. In his ears was a trampling rush, the thunder of the hoofs of the cattle, in career from every quarter of the wide plains to the brow of the hill above him! He fled straight for the castle, scarcely with breath enough to pant.

As he reached the bottom of the valley, the moon peered up over its edge. He had never seen the moon before—except in the daytime, when he had taken her for a thin bright cloud. She was a fresh terror to him—so ghostly! so ghastly! so gruesome!—so knowing as she looked over the top of the her garden-wall upon the world outside! That was the night itself! the darkness alive—and after him! the horror of horrors coming down the sky to curdle his blood, and turn his brain to a cinder! He gave a sob, and made straight for the river, where it ran between the two walls, at the bottom of the garden. He plunged in, struggled through, clambered up the bank, and fell senseless on the grass.

## XII: THE GARDEN

ALTHOUGH Nycteris took care not to stay out long at a time, and used every precaution, she could hardly have escaped discovery so long, had it not been that the strange attacks to which Watho was subject had been more frequent of late, and had at last settled into an illness which kept her to her bed. But whether from an access of caution or from suspicion, Falca, having now to be much with her mistress both day and night, took it at length into her head to fasten the door as often as she went by her usual place of exit; so that one night, when Nycteris pushed, she found, to her surprise and dismay, that the wall pushed her again, and would not let her through; nor with all her searching could she discover wherein lay the cause of the change. Then first she felt the pressure of her prison-walls, and turning, half in despair, groped her way to the picture where she had once seen Falca disappear. There she soon found the spot by pressing upon which the wall yielded. It let her through into a sort of cellar, where was a glimmer of light from a sky whose blue was paled by the moon. From the cellar she got into a long passage, into which the moon was shining, and came to a door. She managed to open it, and, to her great joy, found herself in *the other place*, not on the top of the wall, however, but in the garden she had longed to enter. Noiseless as a fluffy moth she flitted away into the covert of the trees and shrubs, her bare feet welcomed by the softest of carpets, which, by the very touch, her feet knew to be alive, whence it came that it was so sweet and friendly to them. A soft little wind was out among the trees, running now here, now there, like a child that had got its will. She went dancing over the grass, looking behind her at her shadow, as she went. At first she had taken it for a little black creature that made game of her, but when she perceived that it was only where she kept the moon away, and that every tree, however great and grand a creature, had also one of these strange attendants, she soon learned not to mind it, and by and by it became the source of as much amusement to her, as to any kitten its tail. It was long before she was quite at home with the trees, however. At one time they seemed to disapprove of her; at another not even to know she was there, and to be altogether taken up with their own busines. Suddenly, as she went from one to another of them, looking up with awe at the murmuring mystery of their branches and leaves, she spied one a little way off, which was very different from all the rest. It was white, and dark, and sparkling, and spread like a palm—a small slender palm, without much head; and it grew very fast, and sang as it grew. But it never grew any bigger, for just as fast as she could see it growing, it kept falling to pieces. When she got close to it, she discovered that it was a water-tree—made of just such water as she washed with—only it was alive of course, like the river—a different sort of water from that, doubtless, seeing the one crept swiftly along the floor, and the other shot straight up, and fell, and swallowed itself, and rose again. She put her feet into the marble basin, which was the flower-pot in which it grew. It was full of real water, living and cool—so nice, for the night was hot!

But the flowers! ah, the flowers! she was friends with them from the very first. What wonderful crea-tures they were!—and so kind and beautiful—always sending out such colours and such scents—red scent, and white scent, and yellow scent—for the other creatures! The one that was invisible and every-where, took such a quantity of their scents, and car-ried it away! yet they did not seem to mind. It was their talk, to show they were alive, and not painted like those on the walls of her rooms, and on the carpets.

She wandered along down the garden, until she reached the river. Unable then to get any further—for she was a little afraid, and justly, of the swift watery serpent—she dropped on the grassy bank, dipped her feet in the water, and felt it running and pushing against them. For a long time she sat thus, and her

61

bliss seemed complete, as she gazed at the river, and watched the broken picture of the great lamp overhead, moving up one side of the roof, to go down the other.

## XIII: SOMETHING QUITE NEW

A beautiful moth brushed across the great blue eyes of Nycteris. She sprang to her feet to follow it—not in the spirit of the hunter, but of the lover. Her heart—like every heart, if only its fallen sides were cleared away—was an inexhaustible fountain of love: she loved everything she saw. But as she followed the moth, she caught sight of something lying on the bank of the river, and not yet having learned to be afraid of anything, ran straight to see what it was. Reaching it, she stood amazed. Another girl like herself! But what a strange-looking girl!—so curiously dressed too!—and not able to move! Was she dead? Filled suddenly with pity, she sat down, lifted Photogen's head, laid it on her lap, and began stroking his face. Her warm hands brought him to himself. He opened his black eyes, out of which had gone all the fire, and looked up with a strange sound of fear, half moan, half gasp. But when he saw her face, he drew a deep breath, and lay motionless—gazing at her: those blue marvels above him, like a better sky, seemed to side with courage and assuage his terror. At length, in a trembling, awed voice, and a half whisper, he said, "Who are you?"

"I am Nycteris," she answered.

"You are a creature of the darkness, and love the night," he said, his fear beginning to move again.

"I may be a creature of the darkness," she replied. "I hardly know what you mean. But I do not love the night. I love the day—with all my heart; and I sleep all the night long."

62

"How can that be?" said Photogen, rising on his elbow, but dropping his head on her lap again the moment he saw the moon; "— how can it be," he repeated, "when I see your eyes there—wide awake?"

She only smiled and stroked him, for she did not understand him, and thought he did not know what he was saying.

"Was it a dream then?" resumed Photogen, rubbing his eyes. But with that his memory came clear, and he shuddered, and cried, "Oh horrible! horrible! to be turned all at once into a coward! a shameful, contemptible, disgraceful coward! I am ashamed— ashamed—and so frightened! It is all so frightful!"

"What is so frightful?" asked Nycteris, with a smile like that of a mother to her child waked from a bad dream.

"All, all," he answered; "all this darkness and the roaring."

"My dear," said Nycteris, "there is no roaring. How sensitive you must be! What you hear is only the walking of the water, and the running about of the sweetest of all the creatures. She is invisible, and I call her Everywhere, for she goes through all the other creatures and comforts them. Now she is amusing herself, and them too, with shaking them and kissing them, and blowing in their faces. Listen: do you call that roaring? You should hear her when she is rather angry though! I don't know why, but she is sometimes, and then she does roar a little."

"It is so horribly dark!" said Photogen, who, listening while she spoke, had satisfied himself that there was no roaring.

"Dark!" she echoed. "You should be in my room when an earthquake has killed my lamp. I do not understand. How *can* you call this dark? Let me see: yes, you have eyes, and big ones, bigger than Madam

Watho's or Falca's—not so big as mine, I fancy—only I never saw mine. But then—oh yes!—I know now what is the matter! You can't see with them because they are so black. Darkness can't see, of course. Never mind: I will be your eyes, and teach you to see. Look here—at these lovely white things in the grass, and with red sharp points all folded together into one. Oh, I love them so! I could sit looking at them all day, the darlings!"

Photogen looked close at the flowers, and thought he had seen something like them before, but could not make them out. As Nycteris had never seen an open daisy, so had he never seen a closed one.

Thus instinctively Nycteris tried to turn him away from his fear; and the beautiful creature's strange, lovely talk helped not a little to make him forget it.

"You call it dark!" she said again, as if she could not get rid of the absurdity of the idea; "why, I could count every blade of the green hair—I suppose it is what the books call grass—within two yards of me! And just look at the great lamp! It is brighter than usual to-day, and I can't think why you should be frightened, or call it dark!"

As she spoke, she went on stroking his cheeks and hair, and trying to comfort him. But oh how miserable he was! and how plainly he looked it! He was on the point of saying that her great lamp was dreadful to him, looking like a witch, walking in the sleep of death; but he was not so ignorant as Nycteris, and knew even in the moonlight that she was a woman, though he had never seen one so young or so lovely before; and while she comforted his fear, her presence made him the more ashamed of it. Besides, not knowing her nature, he might annoy her, and make her leave him to his misery. He lay still therefore, hardly daring to move: all the little life he had seemed to come from her, and if he were to move, she might move; and if she were to leave him, he must weep like a child.

"How did you come here?" asked Nycteris, taking his face between her hands.

"Down the hill," he answered.

"Where do you sleep?" she asked.

He signed in the direction of the house. She gave a little laugh of delight.

"When you have learned not to be frightened, you will always be wanting to come out with me," she said.

She thought with herself she would ask her presently, when she had come to herself a little, how she had made her escape, for she must, of course, like herself have got out of a cave, in which Watho and Falca had been keeping her.

"Look at the lovely colours," she went on, pointing to a rose-bush, on which Photogen could not see a single flower. "They are far more beautiful—are they not?—than any of the colours upon your walls. And then they are alive, and smell so sweet!"

He wished she would not make him keep opening his eyes to look at things he could not see; and every other moment would start and grasp tight hold of her, as some fresh pang of terror shot into him.

"Come, come, dear!" said Nycteris; "you must not go on this way. You must be a brave girl, and——"

"A girl!" shouted Photogen, and started to his feet in wrath. "If you were a man, I should kill you."

"A man?" repeated Nycteris: "what is that? How could I be that? We are both girls—are we not?"

"No, I am not a girl," he answered; "— although," he added, changing his tone, and casting himself on the ground at her feet, "I have given you too good reason to call me one."

"Oh, I see!" returned Nycteris. "No, of course! you can't be a girl: girls are not afraid—without reason. I understand now: it is because you are not a girl that you are so frightened."

Photogen twisted and writhed upon the grass.

"No, it is not," he said sulkily; "it is this horrible darkness that creeps into me, goes all through me, into the very marrow of my bones—that is what makes me behave like a girl. If only the sun would rise!"

"The sun! what is it?" cried Nycteris, now in her turn conceiving a vague fear.

Then Photogen broke into a rhapsody, in which he vainly sought to forget his.

"It is the soul, the life, the heart, the glory of the universe," he said. "The worlds dance like motes in his beams. The heart of man is strong and brave in his light, and when it departs his courage grows from him—goes with the sun, and he becomes such as you see me now."

"Then that is not the sun?" said Nycteris, thoughtfully, pointing up to the moon.

"That!" cried Photogen, with utter scorn; "I know nothing about *that*, except that it is ugly and horrible. At best it can be only the ghost of a dead sun. Yes, that is it! That is what makes it look so frightful."

"No," said Nycteris, after a long, thoughtful pause; "you must be wrong there. I think the sun is the ghost of a dead moon, and that is how he is so much more splendid as you say.—Is there, then, another big room, where the sun lives in the roof?"

"I do not know what you mean," replied Photogen. "But you mean to be kind, I know, though you should not call a poor fellow in the dark a girl. If you will let me lie here, with my head in your lap, I should like to sleep. Will you watch me, and take care of me?"

"Yes, that I will," answered Nycteris, forgetting all her own danger. So Photogen fell asleep.

## XIV: THE SUN

THERE Nycteris sat, and there the youth lay, all night long, in the heart of the great cone-shadow of the earth, like two Pharaohs in one pyramid. Photogen slept, and slept; and Nycteris sat motionless lest she should wake him, and so betray him to his fear.

The moon rode high in the blue eternity; it was a very triumph of glorious night; the river ran babble-murmuring in deep soft syllables; the fountain kept rushing moonward, and blossoming momently to a great silvery flower, whose petals were for ever falling like snow, but with a continuous musical clash, into the bed of its exhaustion beneath; the wind woke, took a run among the trees, went to sleep, and woke again; the daisies slept on their feet at hers, but she did not know they slept; the roses might well seem awake, for their scent filled the air, but in truth they slept also, and the odour was that of their dreams; the oranges hung like gold lamps in the trees, and their silvery flowers were the souls of their yet unembodied children; the scent of the acacia blooms filled the air like the very odour of the moon herself.

At last, unused to the living air, and weary with sitting so still and so long, Nycteris grew drowsy. The air began to grow cool. It was getting near the time when she too was accustomed to sleep. She closed her eyes just a moment, and nodded—opened them suddenly wide, for she had promised to watch.

In that moment a change had come. The moon had got round, and was fronting her from the west, and she saw that her face was altered, that she had grown pale, as if she too were wan with fear, and from her lofty place espied a coming terror. The light seemed to be dissolving out of her; she was dying— she was going out! And yet everything around looked strangely clear—clearer than ever she had seen any- thing before: how could the lamp be shedding more light when she herself had less? Ah, that was just it! See how faint she looked! It was because the light was forsaking her, and spreading itself over the room, that she grew so thin and pale! She was giving up everything! She was melting away from the roof like a bit of sugar in water.

Nycteris was fast growing afraid, and sought refuge with the face upon her lap. How beautiful the crea- ture was!—what to call it she could not think, for it had been angry when she called it what Watho called her. And, wonder upon wonder! now, even in the cold change that was passing upon the great room, the colour as of a red rose was rising in the wan cheek. What beautiful yellow hair it was that spread over her lap! What great huge breaths the creature took! And what were those curious things it carried? She had seen them on her walls, she was sure.

Thus she talked to herself while the lamp grew paler and paler, and everything kept growing yet clearer. What could it mean? The lamp was dying— going out into the other place of which the creature in her lap had spoken, to be a sun! But why were the things growing clearer before it was yet a sun? That was the point. Was it her growing into a sun that did it? Yes! yes! it was coming death! She knew it, for it was coming upon her also! She felt it coming! What was she about to grow into? Something beautiful, like the creature in her lap? It might be! Anyhow, it must be death; for all her strength was going out of her, while all around her was growing so light she could not bear it! She must be blind soon! Would she be blind or dead first?

For the sun was rushing up behind her. Photogen woke, lifted his head from her lap, and sprang to his feet. His face was one radiant smile. His heart was full of daring—that of the hunter who will creep into the tiger's den. Nycteris gave a cry, covered her face with her hands, and pressed her eyelids close. Then blindly she stretched out her arms to Photogen, crying, "Oh, I am *so* frightened! What is this? It must be death! I don't wish to die yet. I love this room and the old lamp. I do not want the other place! This is terrible. I want to hide. I want to get into the sweet, soft, dark hands of all the other creatures. Ah me! ah me!"

"What is the matter with you, girl?" said Photogen, with the arrogance of all male creatures until they have been taught by the other kind. He stood looking down upon her over his bow, of which he was examining the string. "There is no fear of anything now, child. It is day. The sun is all but up. Look! he will be above the brow of yon hill in one moment more! Good-bye. Thank you for my night's lodging. I'm off. Don't be a goose. If ever I can do anything for you— and all that, you know!"

"Don't leave me: oh, don't leave me!" cried Nycteris. "I am dying! I am dying! I cannot move. The light sucks all the strength out of me. And oh, I am *so* frightened!"

But already Photogen had splashed through the river, holding high his bow that it might not get wet. He rushed across the level, and strained up the opposing hill. Hearing no answer, Nycteris removed her hands. Photogen had reached the top, and the same moment the sunrays alighted upon him: the glory of the king of day crowded blazing upon the golden-haired youth. Radiant as Apollo, he stood in mighty strength, a flashing shape in the midst of flame. He fitted a glowing arrow to a gleaming bow. The arrow parted with a keen musical twang of the bowstring, and Photogen darting after it, vanished with a shout. Up shot Apollo himself, and from his quiver scattered astonishment and exultation. But the brain of poor Nycteris was pierced through and through. She fell down in utter darkness. All around her was a flaming furnace. In despair and feebleness and agony, she crept back, feeling her way with doubt and difficulty and enforced persistence to her cell. When at last the friendly darkness of her chamber folded her about with its cooling and consoling arms, she threw herself on her bed and fell fast asleep. And there she slept on, one alive in a tomb, while Photogen, above in the sun-glory, pursued the buffaloes on the lofty plain, thinking not once of her where she lay dark and forsaken, whose presence had been his refuge, her eyes and her hands his guardians through the night. He was in his glory and his pride; and the darkness and its disgrace had vanished for a time.

## XV: THE COWARD HERO

**B**UT no sooner had the sun reached the noon-stead, than Photogen began to remember the past night in the shadow of that which was at hand, and to remember it with shame. He had proved himself—and not to himself only, but to a girl as well—a coward!—one bold in the daylight, while there was nothing to fear, but trembling like any slave when the night arrived. There was, there must be, something unfair in it! A spell had been cast upon him! He had eaten, he had drunk something that did not agree with courage! In any case he had been taken unprepared! How was he to know what the going down of the sun would be like? It was no wonder he should have been surprised into terror, seeing it was what it was—in its very nature so terrible! Also, one could not see where danger might be coming from! You might be torn in pieces, carried off, or swallowed up, without even seeing where to strike a blow! Every possible excuse he caught at, eager as a self-lover to lighten his self-contempt. That day he astonished the huntsmen—terrified them with his reckless daring—all to prove to himself he was no coward. But nothing eased his shame. One thing only had hope in it—the resolve to encounter the dark in solemn earnest, now that he knew something of what it was. It was nobler to meet a recognized danger than to rush contemptuously into what seemed nothing—nobler still to encounter a nameless horror. He could conquer fear and wipe out disgrace together. For a marksman and swordsman like him, he said, one with his strength and courage, there was but danger. Defeat there was not. He knew the darkness now, and when it came he would meet it as fearless and cool as now he felt himself. And again he said, "We shall see!"

He stood under the boughs of a great beech as the sun was going down, far away over the jagged hills: before it was half down, he was trembling like one of the leaves behind him in the first sigh of the night-wind. The moment the last of the glowing disc vanished, he bounded away in terror to gain the valley, and his fear grew as he ran. Down the side of the hill, an abject creature, he went bounding and rolling and running; fell rather than plunged into the river, and came to himself, as before, lying on the grassy bank in the garden.

But when he opened his eyes, there were no girl-eyes looking down into his; there were only the stars in the waste of the sunless Night—the awful all-enemy he had again dared, but could not encounter. Perhaps the girl was not yet come out of the water! He would try to sleep, for he dared not move, and perhaps when he woke he would find his head on her lap, and the beautiful dark face, with its deep blue eyes, bending over him. But when he woke he found his head on the grass, and although he sprang up with all his courage, such as it was, restored, he did not set out for the chase with such an *elan* as the day before; and, despite the sun-glory in his heart and veins, his hunting was this day less eager; he ate little, and from the first was thoughtful even to sadness. A second time he was defeated and disgraced! Was his courage nothing more than the play of the sunlight on his brain? Was he a mere ball tossed between the light and the dark? Then what a poor contemptible creature he was! But a third chance lay before him. If he failed the third time, he dared not foreshadow what he must then think of himself! It was bad enough now—but then!

Alas! it went no better. The moment the sun was down, he fled as if from a legion of devils.

Seven times in all, he tried to face the coming night in the strength of the past day, and seven times he failed—failed with such increase of failure, with such a growing sense of ignominy, overwhelming at length all the sunny hours and joining night to night, that, what with misery, self-accusation, and loss of confidence, his daylight courage too began to fade, and at length, from exhaustion, from getting wet, and then lying out of doors all night, and night after night,—worst of all, from the consuming of the deathly fear, and the shame of shame, his sleep forsook him, and on the seventh morning, instead of going to the hunt, he crawled into the castle, and went to bed. The grand health, over which the witch had taken such pains, had yielded, and in an hour or two he was moaning and crying out in delirium.

## XVI: AN EVIL NURSE

WATHO was herself ill, as I have said, and was the worse tempered; and, besides, it is a peculiarity of witches, that what works in others to sympathy, works in them to repulsion. Also, Watho had a poor, helpless, rudimentary spleen of a conscience left, just enough to make her uncomfortable, and therefore more wicked. So, when she heard that Photogen was ill, she was angry. Ill, indeed! after all she had done to saturate him with the life of the system, with the solar might itself! He was a wretched failure, the boy! And because he was *her* failure, she was annoyed with him, began to dislike him, grew to hate him. She looked on him as a painter might upon a picture, or a poet upon a poem, which he had only succeeded in getting into an irrecoverable mess. In the hearts of witches, love and hate lie close together, and often tumble over each other. And whether it was that her failure with Photogen foiled also her plans in regard to Nycteris, or that her illness made her yet more of a devil's wife, certainly Watho now got sick of the girl too, and hated to know her about the castle.

She was not too ill, however, to go to poor Photogen's room and torment him. She told him she hated him like a serpent, and hissed like one as she said it, looking very sharp in the nose and chin, and flat in the forehead. Photogen thought she meant to kill him, and hardly ventured to take anything brought him. She ordered every ray of light to be shut out of his room; but by means of this he got a little used to the darkness. She would take one of his arrows, and now tickle him with the feather end of it, now prick him with the point till the blood ran down. What she meant finally I cannot tell, but she brought Photogen speedily to the determination of making his escape from the castle: what he should do then he would think afterwards. Who could tell but he might find his mother somewhere beyond the forest! If it were not for the broad patches of darkness that divided day from day, he would fear nothing!

But now, as he lay helpless in the dark, ever and anon would come dawning through it the face of the lovely creature who on that first awful night nursed him so sweetly: was he never to see her again? If she was, as he had concluded, the nymph of the river, why had she not reappeared? She might have taught him not to fear the night, for plainly she had no fear of it herself! But then, when the day came, she did seem frightened:—why was that, seeing there was nothing to be afraid of then? Perhaps one so much at home in the darkness, was correspondingly afraid of the light! Then his selfish joy at the rising of the sun, blinding him to her condition, had made him behave to her, in ill return for her kindness, as cruelly as Watho behaved to him! How sweet and dear and lovely she was! If there were wild beasts that came out only at night, and were afraid of the light, why should there not be girls too, made the same way—who could not endure the light, as he could not bear the dark-ness? If only he could find her again! Ah, how differ-ently he would behave to her! But alas! perhaps the sun had killed her—melted her—burned her up!—dried her up—that was it, if she was the nymph of the river!

## XVII: WATHO'S WOLF

FROM that dreadful morning Nycteris had never got to be herself again. The sudden light had been almost death to her; and now she lay in the dark with the memory of a terrific sharpness—a something she dared scarcely recall, lest the very thought of it should sting her beyond endurance. But this was as nothing to the pain which the recollection of the rudeness of the shining creature whom she had nursed through his fear caused her; for, the moment his suffering passed over to her, and he was free, the first use he made of his returning strength had been to scorn her! She wondered and wondered; it was all beyond her comprehension.

Before long, Watho was plotting evil against her. The witch was like a sick child weary of his toy: she would pull her to pieces, and see how she liked it. She would set her in the sun, and see her die, like a jelly from the salt ocean cast out on a hot rock. It would be a sight to soothe her wolf-pain. One day, therefore, a little before noon, while Nycteris was in her deepest sleep, she had a darkened litter brought to the door, and in that she made two of her men carry her to the plain above. There they took her out, laid her on the grass, and left her.

Watho watched it all from the top of her high tower, through her telescope; and scarcely was Nycteris left, when she saw her sit up, and the same moment cast herself down again with her face to the ground.

"She'll have a sunstroke," said Watho, "and that'll be the end of her."

Presently, tormented by a fly, a huge-humped buffalo, with great shaggy mane, came galloping along, straight for where she lay. At sight of the thing on the grass, he started, swerved yards aside, stopped dead, and then came slowly up, looking malicious. Nycteris lay quite still, and never even saw the animal.

"Now she'll be trodden to death!" said Watho. "That's the way those creatures do."

When the buffalo reached her, he sniffed at her all over, and went away; then came back, and sniffed again; then all at once went off as if a demon had him by the tail.

Next came a gnu, a more dangerous animal still, and did much the same; then a gaunt wild boar. But no creature hurt her, and Watho was angry with the whole creation.

At length, in the shade of her hair, the blue eyes of Nycteris began to come to themselves a little, and the first thing they saw was a comfort. I have told already how she knew the night-daisies, each a sharp-pointed little cone with a red tip; and once she had parted the rays of one of them, with trembling fingers for she was afraid she was dreadfully rude, and perhaps was hurting it; but she did want, she said to herself, to see what secret it carried so carefully hidden; and she found its golden heart. But now, right under her eyes, inside the veil of her hair, in the sweet twilight of whose blackness she could see it perfectly, stood a daisy with its red tip opened wide into a carmine ring, displaying its heart of gold on a platter of silver. She did not at first recognize it as one of those cones come awake, but a moment's notice revealed what it was. Who then could have been so cruel to the lovely little creature, as to force it open like that, and spread it heart-bare to the terrible death-lamp? Whoever it was, it must be the same that had thrown her out there to be burned to death in its fire! But she had her hair, and could hang her head, and make a small sweet night of her own about her! She tried to bend the daisy down and away from the sun, and to make its petals hang about it like her hair, but she could not. Alas! it was burned and dead already! She did not know that it could not yield to her gentle force because it was drinking life, with all the eagerness of life, from what she called the death-lamp. Oh, how the lamp burned her!

But she went on thinking—she did not know how; and by and by began to reflect that, as there was no roof to the room except that in which the great fire went rolling about, the little Red-tip must have seen the lamp a thousand times, and must know it quite well! and it had not killed it! Nay, thinking about it farther, she began to ask the question whether this, in which she now saw it, might not be its more perfect condition. For not only now did the whole seem perfect, as indeed it did before, but every part showed its own individual perfection as well, which perfection made it capable of combining with the rest into the higher perfection of a whole. The flower was a lamp itself! The golden heart was the light, and the silver border was the alabaster globe, skilfully broken, and spread wide to let out the glory. Yes; the radiant shape was plainly its perfection! If, then, it was the lamp which had opened it into that shape, the lamp could not be unfriendly to it, but must be of its own kind, seeing it made it perfect! And again, when she thought of it, there was clearly no little resemblance between them. What if the flower then was the little great-grandchild of the lamp, and he was loving it all the time? And what if the lamp did not mean to hurt her, only could not help it? The red tips looked as if the flower had some time or other been hurt: what if the lamp was making the best it could of her—opening her out somehow like the flower? She would bear it patiently, and see. But how coarse the colour of the grass was! Perhaps, however, her eyes not being made for the bright lamp, she did not see them as they were! Then she remembered how different were the eyes of the creature that was not a girl and was afraid of the darkness! Ah, if the darkness would only come again, all arms, friendly and soft everywhere about her! She would wait and wait, and bear, and be patient.

She lay so still that Watho did not doubt she had fainted. She was pretty sure she would be dead before the night came to revive her.

## XVIII: REFUGE

IXING her telescope on the motionless form, that she might see it at once when the morning came, Watho went down from the tower to Photogen's room. He was much better by this time, and before she left him, he had resolved to leave the castle that very night. The darkness was terrible indeed, but Watho was worse than even the darkness, and he could not escape in the day. As soon, therefore, as the house seemed still, he tightened his belt, hung to it his hunting-knife, put a flask of wine and some bread in his pocket, and took his bow and arrows. He got from the house, and made his way at once up to the plain. But what with his illness, the terrors of the night, and his dread of the wild beasts, when he got to the level he could not walk a step further, and sat down, thinking it better to die than to live. In spite of his fears, however, sleep contrived to overcome him, and he fell at full length on the soft grass.

He had not slept long when he woke with such a strange sense of comfort and security, that he thought the dawn at least must have arrived. But it was dark night about him. And the sky—no, it was not the sky, but the blue eyes of his naiad looking down upon him! Once more he lay with his head in her lap, and all was well, for plainly the girl feared the darkness as little as he the day.

"Thank you," he said. "You are like live armour to my heart; you keep the fear off me. I have been very ill since then. Did you come up out of the river when you saw me cross?"

"I don't live in the water," she answered. "I live under the pale lamp, and I die under the bright one."

"Ah, yes! I understand now," he returned, "I would not have behaved as I did last time if I had understood; but I thought you were mocking me; and I am so made that I cannot help being frightened at the darkness. I beg your pardon for leaving you as I did, for, as I say, I did not understand. Now I believe you were really frightened. Were you not?"

"I was, indeed," answered Nycteris, "and shall be again. But why you should be, I cannot in the least understand. You must know how gentle and sweet the darkness is, how kind and friendly, how soft and velvety! It holds you to its bosom and loves you. A little while ago, I lay faint and dying under your hot lamp.—What is it you call it?"

"The sun," murmured Photogen: "how I wish he would make haste!"

"Ah! do not wish that. Do not, for my sake, hurry him. I can take care of you from the darkness, but I have no one to take care of me from the light.—As I was telling you, I lay dying in the sun. All at once I drew a deep breath. A cool wind came and ran over my face. I looked up. The torture was gone, for the death-lamp itself was gone. I hope he does not die and grow brighter yet. My terrible headache was all gone, and my sight was come back. I felt as if I were new made. But I did not get up at once, for I was tired still. The grass grew cool about me, and turned soft in colour. Something wet came upon it, and it was now so pleasant to my feet, that I rose and ran about. And when I had been running about a long time, all at once I found you lying, just as I had been lying a little while before. So I sat down beside you to take care of you, till your life—and my death— should come again."

"How good you are, you beautiful creature!—Why, you forgave me before ever I asked you!" cried Photogen.

Thus they fell a-talking, and he told her what he knew of his history, and she told him what she knew of hers, and they agreed they must get away from Watho as far as ever they could.

"And we must set out at once," said Nycteris.

"The moment the morning comes," returned Photogen.

"We must not wait for the morning," said Nycteris, "for then I shall not be able to move, and what would you do the next night? Besides, Watho sees best in the daytime. Indeed, you must come now, Photogen.—You must."

"I can not; I dare not," said Photogen. "I cannot move. If I but lift my head from your lap, the very sickness of terror seizes me."

"I shall be with you," said Nycteris soothingly. "I will take care of you till your dreadful sun comes, and then you may leave me, and go away as fast as you can. Only please put me in a dark place first, if there is one to be found."

"I will never leave you again, Nycteris," cried Photogen. "Only wait till the sun comes, and brings me back my strength, and we will go away together, and never, never part any more."

"No, no," persisted Nycteris; "we must go now. And you must learn to be strong in the dark as well as in the day, else you will always be only half brave. I have begun already—not to fight your sun, but to try to get at peace with him, and understand what he really is, and what he means with me—whether to hurt me or to make the best of me. You must do the same with my darkness."

"But you don't know what mad animals there are away there towards the south," said Photogen. "They have huge green eyes, and they would eat you up like a bit of celery, you beautiful creature!"

"Come, come! you must," said Nycteris, "or I shall have to pretend to leave you, to make you come. I

80

have seen the green eyes you speak of, and I will take care of you from them."

"You! How can you do that? If it were day now, I could take care of you from the worst of them. But as it is, I can't even see them for this abominable darkness. I could not see your lovely eyes but for the light that is in them; that lets me see straight into heaven through them. They are windows into the very heaven beyond the sky. I believe they are the very place where the stars are made."

"You come then, or I shall shut them," said Nycteris, "and you shan't see them any more till you are good. Come. If you can't see the wild beasts, I can."

"You can! and you ask me to come!" cried Photogen.

"Yes," answered Nycteris. "And more than that, I see them long before they can see me, so that I am able to take care of you."

"But how?" persisted Photogen. "You can't shoot with bow and arrow, or stab with a hunting-knife."

"No, but I can keep out of the way of them all. Why, just when I found you, I was having a game with two or three of them at once. I see, and scent them too, long before they are near me—long before they can see or scent me."

"You don't see or scent any now, do you?" said Photogen, uneasily, rising on his elbow.

"No—none at present. I will look," replied Nycteris, and sprang to her feet.

"Oh, oh! do not leave me—not for a moment," cried Photogen, straining his eyes to keep her face in sight through the darkness.

"Be quiet, or they will hear you," she returned. "The wind is from the south, and they cannot scent us. I have found out all about that. Ever since the dear dark came, I have been amusing myself with them, getting every now and then just into the edge of the wind, and letting one have a sniff of me."

81

"Oh, horrible!" cried Photogen. "I hope you will not insist on doing so any more. What was the consequence?"

"Always, the very instant, he turned with flashing eyes, and bounded towards me—only he could not see me, you must remember. But my eyes being so much better than his, I could see him perfectly well, and would run away round him until I scented him, and then I knew he could not find me anyhow. If the wind were to turn, and run the other way now, there might be a whole army of them down upon us, leaving no room to keep out of their way. You had better come."

She took him by the hand. He yielded and rose, and she led him away. But his steps were feeble, and as the night went on, he seemed more and more ready to sink.

"Oh dear! I am so tired! and so frightened!" he would say.

"Lean on me," Nycteris would return, putting her arm round him, or patting his cheek. "Take a few steps more. Every step away from the castle is clear gain. Lean harder on me. I am quite strong and well now."

So they went on. The piercing night-eyes of Nycteris descried not a few pairs of green ones gleaming like holes in the darkness, and many a round she made to keep far out of their way; but she never said to Photogen she saw them. Carefully she kept him off the uneven places, and on the softest and smoothest of the grass, talking to him gently all the way as they went—of the lovely flowers and the stars—how comfortable the flowers looked, down in their green beds, and how happy the stars up in their blue beds!

When the morning began to come, he began to grow better, but was dreadfully tired with walking instead of sleeping, especially after being so long ill.

Nycteris too, what with supporting him, what with growing fear of the light which was beginning to ooze out of the east, was very tired. At length, both equally exhausted, neither was able to help the other. As if by consent they stopped. Embracing each the other, they stood in the midst of the wide grassy land, neither of them able to move a step, each supported only by the leaning weakness of the other, each ready to fall if the other should move. But while the one grew weaker still, the other had begun to grow stronger. When the tide of the night began to ebb, the tide of the day began to flow; and now the sun was rushing to the horizon, borne upon its foaming billows. And ever as he came, Photogen revived. At last the sun shot up into the air, like a bird from the hand of the Father of Lights. Nycteris gave a cry of pain, and hid her face in her hands.

"Oh me!" she sighed; "I am *so* frightened! The terrible light stings so!"

But the same instant, through her blindness, she heard Photogen give a low exultant laugh, and the next felt herself caught up: she who all night long had tended and protected him like a child, was now in his arms, borne along like a baby, with her head lying on his shoulder. But she was the greater, for, suffering more, she feared nothing.


## XIX: THE WEREWOLF

AT the very moment when Photogen caught up Nycteris, the telescope of Watho was angrily sweeping the table-land. She swung it from her in rage, and running to her room, shut herself up. There she anointed herself from top to toe with a certain ointment; shook down her long red hair, and tied it round her waist; then began to dance, whirling round and round faster and faster, growing angrier and angrier, until she was foaming at the mouth with fury. When Falca went looking for her, she could not find her anywhere.

As the sun rose, the wind slowly changed and went round, until it blew straight from the north. Photogen and Nycteris were drawing near the edge of the forest, Photogen still carrying Nycteris, when she moved a little on his shoulder uneasily, and murmured in his ear,

"I smell a wild beast—that way, the way the wind is coming."

Photogen turned, looked back towards the castle, and saw a dark speck on the plain. As he looked, it grew larger: it was coming across the grass with the speed of the wind. It came nearer and nearer. It looked long and low, but that might be because it was running at a great stretch. He set Nycteris down under a tree, in the black shadow of its bole, strung his bow, and picked out his heaviest, longest, sharpest arrow. Just as he set the notch on the string, he saw that the creature was a tremendous wolf, rushing straight at him. He loosened his knife in its sheath, drew another arrow half-way from the quiver, lest the first should fail, and took his aim—at a good distance, to leave time for a second chance. He shot. The arrow rose, flew straight, descended, struck the beast, and started again into the air, doubled like a letter V. Quickly Photogen snatched the other, shot, cast his bow from him, and drew his knife. But the arrow was in the brute's chest, up to the feather; it tumbled heels over head with a great thud of its back on the earth, gave a groan, made a struggle or two, and lay stretched out motionless.

"I've killed it, Nycteris," cried Photogen. "It is a great red wolf."

"Oh, thank you!" answered Nycteris feebly from behind the tree. "I was sure you would. I was not a bit afraid."

Photogen went up to the wolf. It *was* a monster! But he was vexed that his first arrow had behaved so badly, and was the less willing to lose the one that had done him such good service: with a long and strong pull, he drew it from the brute's chest. Could he believe his eyes? There lay—no wolf, but Watho, with her hair tied round her waist! The foolish witch had made herself invulnerable, as she supposed, but had forgotten that, to torment Photogen therewith, she had handled one of his arrows. He ran back to Nycteris and told her.

She shuddered and wept, and would not look.

## XX: ALL IS WELL

HERE was now no occasion to fly a step farther. Neither of them feared any one but Watho. They left her there, and went back. A great cloud came over the sun, and rain began to fall heavily, and Nycteris was much refreshed, grew able to see a little, and with Photogen's help walked gently over the cool, wet grass.

They had not gone far before they met Fargu and the other huntsmen. Photogen told them he had killed a great red wolf, and it was Madam Watho. The huntsmen looked grave, but gladness shone through.

"Then," said Fargu, "I will go and bury my mistress."

But when they reached the place, they found she was already buried—in the maws of sundry birds and beasts which had made their breakfast of her.

Then Fargu, overtaking them, would, very wisely, have Photogen go to the king, and tell him the whole story. But Photogen, yet wiser than Fargu, would not set out until he had married Nycteris; "for then," he said, "the king himself can't part us; and if ever two people couldn't do the one without the other, those two are Nycteris and I. She has got to teach me to be

85

a brave man in the dark, and I have got to look after her until she can bear the heat of the sun, and he helps her to see, instead of blinding her."

They were married that very day. And the next day they went together to the king, and told him the whole story. But whom should they find at the court but the father and mother of Photogen, both in high favour with the king and queen. Aurora nearly died for joy, and told them all how Watho had lied, and made her believe her child was dead.

No one knew anything of the father or mother of Nycteris; but when Aurora saw in the lovely girl her own azure eyes shining through night and its clouds, it made her think strange things, and wonder how even the wicked themselves may be a link to join together the good. Through Watho, the mothers, who had never seen each other, had changed eyes in their children.

The king gave them the castle and lands of Watho, and there they lived and taught each other for many years that were not long. But hardly had one of them passed, before Nycteris had come to love the day best, because it was the clothing and crown of Photogen, and she saw that the day was greater than the night, and the sun more lordly than the moon; and Photogen had come to love the night best, because it was the mother and home of Nycteris.

"But who knows," Nycteris would say to Photogen, "that, when we go out, we shall not go into a day as much greater than your day as your day is greater than my night?"

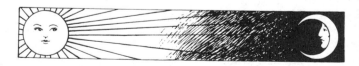

# THE SHAPOWS

OLD Ralph Rinkelmann made his living by comic sketches, and all but lost it again by tragic poems. So he was just the man to be chosen king of the fairies, for in Fairyland the sovereignty is elective.

It is no doubt very strange that fairies should desire to have a mortal king; but the fact is, that with all their knowledge and power, they cannot get rid of the feeling that some men are greater than they are, though they can neither fly nor play tricks. So at such times as there happen to be twice the usual number of sensible electors, such a man as Ralph Rinkelmann gets to be chosen.

They did not mean to insist on his residence; for they needed his presence only on special occasions. But they must get hold of him somehow, first of all, in order to make him king. Once he was crowned, they could get him as often as they pleased; but before this ceremony, there was a difficulty. For it is only between life and death that the fairies have power over grown-up mortals, and can carry them off to their country. So they had to watch for an opportunity.

Nor had they to wait long. For old Ralph was taken dreadfully ill; and while hovering between life and death, they carried him off, and crowned him king of Fairyland. But after he was crowned, it was no wonder, considering the state of his health, that he

Reprinted from *Adela Cathcart* (1864).

should not be able to sit quite upright on the throne of Fairyland; or that, in consequence, all the gnomes and goblins, and ugly, cruel things that live in the holes and corners of the kingdom, should take advantage of his condition, and run quite wild, playing him, king as he was, all sorts of tricks; crowding about his throne, climbing up the steps, and actually scrambling and quarrelling like mice about his ears and eyes, so that he could see and think of nothing

else. But I am not going to tell anything more about this part of his adventures just at present. By strong and sustained efforts, he succeeded, after much trouble and suffering, in reducing his rebellious subjects to order. They all vanished to their respective holes and corners; and King Ralph, coming to himself, found himself in his bed, half propped up with pillows.

But the room was full of dark creatures, which gambolled about in the firelight in such a strange, huge, though noiseless fashion, that he thought at first that some of his rebellious goblins had not been subdued with the rest, but had followed him beyond the bounds of Fairyland into his own private house, in London. How else could these mad, grotesque hippopotamus-calves make their ugly appearance in Ralph Rinkelmann's bedroom? But he soon found out that although they were like the underground goblins, they were very different as well, and would require quite different treatment. He felt convinced that they were his subjects too, but that he must have overlooked them somehow at his late coronation—if indeed they had been present; for he could not recollect that he had seen anything just like them before. He resolved, therefore, to pay particular attention to their habits, ways, and characters; else he saw plainly that they would soon be too much for him; as indeed this intrusion into his chamber, where Mrs. Rinkelmann, who must be queen if he was king, sat taking some tea by the fireside, evidently foreshadowed. But she, perceiving that he was looking about him with a more composed expression than his face had worn for many days, started up, and came quickly and quietly to his side, and her face was bright with gladness. Whereupon the fire burned up more cheerily; and the figures became more composed and respectful in their behaviour, retreating towards the wall like well-trained attendants. Then the king of Fairyland had some tea and dry toast, and leaning back on his pillows, nearly fell asleep; but not quite, for he still watched the intruders.

Presently the queen left the room to give some of the young princes and princesses their tea; and the fire burned lower, and behold, the figures grew as black and as mad in their gambols as ever! Their favourite games seemed to be *Hide and Seek; Touch and Go; Grin and Vanish:* and many other such; and all in the king's bedchamber, too; so that it was quite alarming. It was almost as bad as if the house had been haunted by certain creatures which shall be nameless in a fairy story, because with them Fairyland will not willingly have much to do.

"But it is a mercy that they have their slippers on!" said the king to himself; for his head ached.

As he lay back, with his eyes half shut and half open, too tired to pay longer attention to their games, but, on the whole, considerably more amused than offended with the liberties they took, for they seemed good-natured creatures, and more frolicsome than positively ill-mannered, he became suddenly aware that two of them had stepped forward from the walls, upon which, after the manner of great spiders, most of them preferred sprawling, and now stood in the middle of the floor at the foot of his majesty's bed, becking and bowing and ducking in the most grotesquely obsequious manner; while every now and then they turned solemnly round upon one heel, evidently considering that motion the highest token of homage they could show.

"What do you want?" said the king.

"That it may please your majesty to be better acquainted with us," answered they. "We are your majesty's subjects."

"I know you are. I shall be most happy," answered the king.

"We are not what your majesty takes us for, though. We are not so foolish as your majesty thinks us."

"It is impossible to take you for anything that I know of," rejoined the king, who wished to make them talk, and said whatever came uppermost;—"for soldiers, sailors, or anything: you will not stand still long enough. I suppose you really belong to the fire brigade; at least, you keep putting its light out."

"Don't jest, please your majesty." And as they said the words—for they both spoke at once throughout the interview—they performed a grave somerset towards the king.

"Not jest!" retorted he; "and with you? Why, you do nothing but jest. What are you?"

"The Shadows, sire. And when we do jest, sire, we always jest in earnest. But perhaps your majesty does not see us distinctly."

"I see you perfectly well," returned the king.

"Permit me, however," rejoined one of the Shadows; and as he spoke he approached the king; and lifting a dark forefinger, he drew it lightly but carefully across the ridge of his forehead, from temple to temple. The king felt the soft gliding touch go, like water, into every hollow, and over the top of every height of that mountain-chain of thought. He had involuntarily closed his eyes during the operation, and when he unclosed them again, as soon as the finger was withdrawn, he found that they were opened in more senses than one. The room appeared to have extended itself on all sides, till he could not exactly see where the walls were; and all about it stood the Shadows motionless. They were tall and solemn; rather awful, indeed, in their appearance, notwithstanding many remarkable traits of grotesqueness, for they looked just like the pictures of Puritans drawn by Cavaliers, with long arms, and very long, thin legs, from which hung large loose feet, while in their countenances length of chin and nose predominated. The solemnity of their mien, however, overcame all the oddity of their form, so that they were very *eerie* indeed to look at, dressed as they all were in funereal black. But a single glance was all that the king was allowed to have; for the former operator waved his dusky palm across his vision, and once more the king saw only the fire-lighted walls, and dark shapes flickering about upon them. The two who had spoken for the rest seemed likewise to have vanished. But at last the king discovered them, standing one on each side of the fireplace. They kept close to the chimney-wall, and talked to each other across the length of the chimney-piece; thus avoiding the direct rays of the fire, which, though light is necessary to their appearing to human eyes, do not agree with them at all—much less give birth to them, as the king was soon to learn. After a few minutes they again approached the bed, and spoke thus:—

"It is now getting dark, please your majesty. We mean, out of doors in the snow. Your majesty may see, from where he is lying, the cold light of its great winding-sheet—a famous carpet for the Shadows to dance upon, your majesty. All our brothers and sisters will be at church now, before going to their night's work."

"Do they always go to church before they go to work?"

"They always go to church first."

"Where is the church?"

"In Iceland. Would your majesty like to see it?"

"How can I go and see it, when, as you know very well, I am ill in bed? Besides, I should be sure to take cold in a frosty night like this, even if I put on the blankets, and took the feather-bed for a muff."

A sort of quivering passed over their faces, which seemed to be their mode of laughing. The whole shape of the face shook and fluctuated as if it had been some dark fluid; till, by slow degrees of gathering calm, it settled into its former rest. Then one of them drew aside the curtains of the bed, and the window-curtains not having been yet drawn, the king beheld the white glimmering night outside, struggling with the heaps of darkness that tried to quench it; and the heavens full of stars, flashing and sparkling like live jewels. The other Shadow went towards the fire and vanished in it.

Scores of Shadows immediately began an insane dance all about the room; disappearing, one after the other, through the uncovered window, and gliding darkly away over the face of the white snow; for the window looked at once on a field of snow. In a few moments the room was quite cleared of them; but instead of being relieved by their absence, the king felt immediately as if he were in a dead-house, and could hardly breathe for the sense of emptiness and desolation that fell upon him. But as he lay looking out on the snow, which stretched blank and wide before him, he spied in the distance a long dark line which drew nearer and nearer, and showed itself at last to be all the Shadows, walking in a double row, and carrying in the midst of them something like a bier. They vanished under the window, but soon reappeared, having somehow climbed up the wall of the house; for they entered in perfect order by the window, as if melting through the transparency of the glass.

They still carried the bier or litter. It was covered with richest furs, and skins of gorgeous wild beasts, whose eyes were replaced by sapphires and emeralds, that glittered and gleamed in the fire and snow light. The outermost skin sparkled with frost, but the inside ones were soft and warm and dry as the down under a swan's wing. The Shadows approached the

bed, and set the litter upon it. Then a number of them
brought a huge fur robe, and wrapping it round the
king, laid him on the litter in the midst of the furs.
Nothing could be more gentle and respectful than the
way in which they moved him; and he never thought
of refusing to go. Then they put something on his
head, and, lifting the litter, carried him once round
the room, to fall into order. As he passed the mirror
he saw that he was covered with royal ermine, and
that his head wore a wonderful crown of gold, set
with none but red stones: rubies and carbuncles and
garnets, and others whose names he could not tell,
glowed gloriously around his head, like the salaman-
drine essence of all the Christmas fires over the world.
A sceptre lay beside him—a rod of ebony, sur-
mounted by a cone-shaped diamond, which, cut in
a hundred facets, flashed all the hues of the rainbow,
and threw coloured gleams on every side, that looked
like Shadows too, but more ethereal than those that
bore him. Then the Shadows rose gently to the window, passed through it, and sinking slowly upon the
field of outstretched snow, commenced an orderly
gliding rather than march along the frozen surface.
They took it by turns to bear the king, as they sped
with the swiftness of thought, in a straight line towards the north. The pole-star rose above their heads
with visible rapidity; for indeed they moved quite as
fast as sad thoughts, though not with all the speed
of happy desires. England and Scotland slid past the
litter of the king of the Shadows. Over rivers and
lakes they skimmed and glided. They climbed the
high mountains, and crossed the valleys with a fearless bound; till they came to John-o'-Groat's house
and the Northern Sea. The sea was not frozen; for all
the stars shone as clear out of the deeps below as
they shone out of the deeps above; and as the bearers
slid along the blue-gray surface, with never a furrow

in their track, so pure was the water beneath, that the king saw neither surface, bottom, nor substance to it, and seemed to be gliding only through the blue sphere of heaven, with the stars above him, and the stars below him, and between the stars and him nothing but an emptiness, where, for the first time in his life, his soul felt that it had room enough.

At length they reached the rocky shores of Iceland. There they landed, still pursuing their journey. All this time the king felt no cold; for the red stones in his crown kept him warm, and the emerald and sapphire eyes of the wild beasts kept the frosts from settling upon his litter.

Oftentimes upon their way they had to pass through forests, caverns, and rock-shadowed paths, where it was so dark that at first the king feared he should lose his Shadows altogether. But as soon as they entered such places, the diamond in his sceptre began to shine, and glow, and flash, sending out streams of light of all the colours that painter's soul could dream of; in which light the Shadows grew livelier and stronger than ever, speeding through the dark ways with an all but blinding swiftness. In the light of the diamond, too, some of their forms became more simple and human, while others seemed only to break out into a yet more untamable absurdity. Once, as they passed through a cave, the king actually saw some of their eyes—strange shadow-eyes: he had never seen any of their eyes before. But at the same moment when he saw their eyes, he knew their faces too, for they turned them full upon him for an instant; and the other Shadows, catching sight of these, shrank and shivered, and nearly vanished. Lovely faces they were; but the king was very thoughtful after he saw them, and continued rather troubled all the rest of the journey. He could not account for those faces being there, and the faces of Shadows, too, with living eyes.

But he soon found that amongst the Shadows a man must learn never to be surprised at anything; for if he does not, he will soon grow quite stupid, in consequence of the endless recurrence of surprises.

At last they climbed up the bed of a little stream, and then, passing through a narrow rocky defile, came out suddenly upon the side of a mountain, overlooking a blue frozen lake in the very heart of mighty hills. Overhead, the *aurora borealis* was shivering and flashing like a battle of ten thousand spears. Underneath, its beams passed faintly over the blue ice and the sides of the snow-clad mountains, whose tops shot up like huge icicles all about, with here and there a star sparkling on the very tip of one. But as the northern lights in the sky above, so wavered and quivered, and shot hither and thither, the Shadows on the suface of the lake below; now gathering in groups, and now shivering asunder; now covering the whole surface of the lake, and anon condensed into one dark knot in the centre. Every here and there on the white mountains might be seen two or three shooting away towards the tops, to vanish beyond them, so that the number was gradually, though not visibly, diminishing.

"Please your majesty," said the Shadows, "this is our church—the Church of the Shadows."

And so saying, the king's body-guard set down the litter upon a rock, and plunged into the multitudes below. They soon returned, however, and bore the king down into the middle of the lake. All the Shadows came crowding round him, respectfully but fearlessly; and sure never such a grotesque assembly revealed itself before to mortal eyes. The king had seen all kinds of gnomes, goblins, and kobolds at his coronation; but they were quite rectilinear figures compared with the insane lawlessness of form in which the Shadows rejoiced; and the wildest gambols of the former were orderly dances of ceremony beside the apparently aimless and wilful contortions of figure, and metamorphoses of shape, in which the latter indulged. They retained, however, all the time, to the surprise of the king, an identity, each of his own type, inexplicably perceptible through every change. Indeed, this preservation of the primary idea of each form was more wonderful than the bewildering and ridiculous alterations to which the form itself was every moment subjected.

"What are you?" said the king, leaning on his elbow, and looking around him.

"The Shadows, your majesty," answered several voices at once.

"What Shadows?"

"The human Shadows. The Shadows of men, and women, and their children."

"Are you not the shadows of chairs and tables, and pokers and tongs, just as well?"

At this question a strange jarring commotion went through the assembly with a shock. Several of the figures shot up as high as the aurora, but instantly settled down again to human size, as if overmastering their feelings, out of respect to him who had roused them. One who had bounded to the highest visible icy peak, and as suddenly returned, now elbowed his way through the rest, and made himself spokesman for them during the remaining part of the dialogue.

"Excuse our agitation, your majesty," said he. "I see your majesty has not yet thought proper to make himself acquainted with our nature and habits."

"I wish to do so now," replied the king.

"We are the Shadows," repeated the Shadow, solemnly.

"Well?" said the king.

"We do not often appear to men."

"Ha!" said the king.

"We do not belong to the sunshine at all. We go through it unseen, and only by a passing chill do men recognize an unknown presence."

"Ha!" said the king again.

"It is only in the twilight of the fire, or when one man or woman is alone with a single candle, or when any number of people are all feeling the same thing at once, making them one, that we show ourselves, and the truth of things."

"Can that be true that loves the night?" said the king.

"The darkness is the nurse of light," answered the Shadow.

"Can that be true which mocks at forms?" said the king.

"Truth rides abroad in shapeless storms," answered the Shadow.

"Ha! ha!" thought Ralph Rinkelmann, "it rhymes. The Shadow caps my questions with his answers. Very strange!" And he grew thoughtful again.

The Shadow was the first to resume.

"Please your majesty, may we present our petition?"

"By all means," replied the king. "I am not well enough to receive it in proper state."

"Never mind, your majesty. We do not care for much ceremony; and indeed none of us are quite well at present. The subject of our petition weighs upon us."

"Go on," said the king.

"Sire," began the Shadow, "our very existence is in danger. The various sorts of artificial light, both in houses and in men, women, and children, threaten to end our being. The use and the disposition of gas-lights, especially high in the centres, blind the eyes by which alone we can be perceived. We are all but banished from towns. We are driven into villages and lonely houses, chiefly old farm-houses, out of which, even, our friends the fairies are fast disappearing. We therefore petition our king, by the power of his art, to restore us to our rights in the house itself, and in the hearts of its inhabitants."

"But," said the king, "you frighten the children."

"Very seldom, your majesty; and then only for their good. We seldom seek to frighten anybody. We mostly want to make people silent and thoughtful; to awe them a little, your majesty."

"You are much more likely to make them laugh," said the king.

"Are we?" said the Shadow.

And approaching the king one step, he stood quite still for a moment. The diamond of the king's sceptre shot out a vivid flame of violet light, and the king stared at the Shadow in silence, and his lip quivered. He never told what he saw then; but he would say:

"Just fancy what it might be if *some* flitting thoughts were to persist in staying to be looked at."

"It is only," resumed the Shadow, "when our thoughts are not fixed upon any particular object, that our bodies are subject to all the vagaries of elemental influences. Generally, amongst worldly men and frivolous women, we only attach ourselves to some article of furniture or of dress; and they never doubt that we are mere foolish and vague results of the dashing of the waves of the light against the solid forms of which their houses are full. We do not care to tell them the truth, for they would never see it. But let the worldly man—or the frivolous woman—and then—"

At each of the pauses indicated, the mass of Shadows throbbed and heaved with emotion; but they soon settled again into comparative stillness. Once more the Shadow addressed himself to speak. But suddenly they all looked up, and the king, following their gaze, saw that the aurora had begun to pale.

"The moon is rising," said the Shadow. "As soon as she looks over the mountains into the valley, we must be gone, for we have plenty to do by the moon: we are powerful in her light. But if your majesty will come here to-morrow night, your majesty may learn a great deal more about us, and judge for himself whether it be fit to accord our petition; for then will be our grand annual assembly, in which we report to our chiefs the things we have attempted, and the good or bad success we have had."

"If you send for me," returned the king, "I will come."

Ere the Shadow could reply, the tip of the moon's crescent horn peeped up from behind an icy pinnacle, and one slender ray fell on the lake. It shone upon no Shadows. Ere the eye of the king could again seek the earth after beholding the first brightness of the moon's resurrection, they had vanished; and the surface of the lake glittered cold and blue in the pale moonlight.

There the king lay, alone in the midst of the frozen lake, with the moon staring at him. But at length he heard from somewhere a voice that he knew.

"Will you take another cup of tea, dear?" said Mrs. Rinkelmann.

And Ralph, coming slowly to himself, found that he was lying in his own bed.

"Yes, I will," he answered; "and rather a large piece of toast, if you please; for I have been a long journey since I saw you last."

"He has not come to himself quite," said Mrs. Rinkelmann, between her and herself.

"You would be rather surprised," continued Ralph, "if I told you where I have been."

"I dare say I should," responded his wife.

*Ralph saw a great shadow shaking its fist
at him from the end of a preposterous arm.*

"Then I will tell you," rejoined Ralph.

But at that moment a great Shadow bounced out of the fire with a single huge leap, and covered the whole room. Then it settled in one corner, and Ralph saw it shaking its fist at him from the end of a preposterous arm. So he took the hint, and held his peace. And it was as well for him. For I happen to know something about the Shadows too; and I know that if he had told his wife all about it just then, they would not have sent for him the following evening.

But as the king, after finishing his tea and toast, lay and looked about him, the shadows dancing in his room seemed to him odder and more inexplicable than ever. The whole chamber was full of mystery. So it generally was, but now it was more mysterious than ever. After all that he had seen in the Shadow-church, his own room and its shadows were yet more wonderful and unintelligible than those.

This made it the more likely that he had seen a true vision; for instead of making common things look commonplace, as a false vision would have done, it had made common things disclose the wonderful that was in them.

"The same applies to all art as well," thought Ralph Rinkelmann.

The next afternoon, as the twilight was growing dusky, the king lay wondering whether or not the Shadows would fetch him again. He wanted very much to go, for he had enjoyed the journey exceedingly, and he longed, besides, to hear some of the Shadows tell their stories. But the darkness grew deeper and deeper, and the Shadows did not come. The cause was, that Mrs. Rinkelmann sat by the fire in the gloaming; and they could not carry off the king while she was there. Some of them tried to frighten her away by playing the oddest pranks on the walls, the floor, and ceiling; but altogether without effect:

the queen only smiled, for she had a good conscience. Suddenly, however, a dreadful scream was
heard from the nursery, and Mrs. Rinkelmann rushed
up-stairs to see what was the matter. No sooner had
she gone than the two warders of the chimney-cor-
ners stepped out into the middle of the room, and
said, in a low voice, —

"Is your majesty ready?"

"Have you no hearts?" said the king; "or are they
as black as your faces? Did you not hear the child
scream? I must know what is the matter with her
before I go."

"Your majesty may keep his mind easy on that
point," replied the warders. "We had tried everything
we could think of to get rid of her majesty the queen,
but without effect. So a young madcap Shadow, half
against the will of the older ones of us, slipped up-
stairs into the nursery; and has, no doubt, succeeded
in appalling the baby, for he is very lithe and long-
legged. —Now, your majesty."

"I will have no such tricks played in my nursery,"
said the king, rather angrily. "You might put the child
beside itself."

"Then there would be twins, your majesty. And we
rather like twins."

"None of your miserable jesting! You might put the
child out of her wits."

"Impossible, sire; for she has not got into them
yet."

"Go away," said the king.

"Forgive us, your majesty. Really, it will do the
child good; for that Shadow will, all her life, be to her
a symbol of what is ugly and bad. When she feels in
danger of hating or envying any one, that Shadow will
come back to her mind and make her shudder."

"Very well," said the king. "I like that. Let us go."

The Shadows went through the same ceremonies

103

and preparations as before; during which, the young Shadow before-mentioned contrived to make such grimaces as kept the baby in terror, and the queen in the nursery, till all was ready. Then with a bound that doubled him up against the ceiling, and a kick of his legs six feet out behind him, he vanished through the nursery door, and reached the king's bed-chamber just in time to take his place with the last who were melting through the window in the rear of the litter, and settling down upon the snow beneath. Away they went as before, a gliding blackness over the white carpet. And it was Christmas-eve.

When they came in sight of the mountain-lake, the king saw that it was crowded over its whole surface with a changeful intermingling of Shadows. They were all talking and listening alternately, in pairs, trios, and groups of every size. Here and there, large companies were absorbed in attention to one elevated above the rest, not in a pulpit, or on a platform, but on the stilts of his own legs, elongated for the nonce. The aurora, right overhead, lighted up the lake and the sides of the mountains, by sending down from the zenith, nearly to the surface of the lake, great folded vapours, luminous with all the colours of a faint rainbow.

Many, however, as the words were that passed on all sides, not a shadow of a sound reached the ears of the king: the shadow-speech could not enter his corporeal organs. One of his guides, however, seeing that the king wanted to hear and could not, went through a strange manipulation of his head and ears; after which he could hear perfectly, though still only the voice to which, for the time, he directed his attention. This, however, was a great advantage, and one which the king longed to carry back with him to the world of men.

The king now discovered that this was not merely the church of the Shadows, but their news-exchange at the same time. For, as the Shadows have no writing or printing, the only way in which they can make each other aquainted with their doings and thinkings, is to meet and talk at this word-mart and parliament of shades. And as, in the world, people read their favourite authors, and listen to their favourite speakers, so here the Shadows seek their favourite Shadows, listen to their adventures, and hear generally what they have to say.

Feeling quite strong, the king rose and walked about amongst them, wrapped in his ermine robe, with his red crown on his head, and his diamond sceptre in his hand. Every group of Shadows to which he drew near, ceased talking as soon as they saw him approach: but at a nod they went on again directly, conversing and relating and commenting, as if no one was there of other kind or of higher rank than themselves. So the king heard a good many stories. At some of them he laughed, and at some of them he cried. But if the stories that the Shadows told were printed, they would make a book that no publisher could produce fast enough to satisfy the buyers. I will record some of the things that the king heard, for he told them to me soon after. In fact, I was for some time his private secretary.

"I made him confess before a week was over," said a gloomy old Shadow.

"But what was the good of that?" rejoined a pert young one. "That could not undo what was done."

"Yes, it could."

"What! bring the dead to life?"

"No; but comfort the murderer. I could not bear to see the pitiable misery he was in. He was far happier with the rope round his neck, than he was with the purse in his pocket. I saved him from killing himself too."

"How did you make him confess?"

105

"Only by wallowing on the wall a little."

"How could that make him tell?"

"*He* knows."

The Shadow was silent; and the king turned to another, who was preparing to speak.

"I made a fashionable mother repent."

"How?" broke from several voices, in whose sound was mingled a touch of incredulity.

"Only by making a little coffin on the wall," was the reply.

"Did the fashionable mother confess too?"

"She had nothing more to confess than everybody knew."

"What did everybody know then?"

"That she might have been kissing a living child, when she followed a dead one to the grave.—The next will fare better."

"I put a stop to a wedding," said another.

"Horrid shade!" remarked a poetic imp.

"How?" said others. "Tell us how."

"Only by throwing a darkness, as if from the branch of a sconce, over the forehead of a fair girl.—They are not married yet, and I do not think they will be. But I loved the youth who loved her. How he started! It was a revelation to him."

"But did it not deceive him?"

"Quite the contrary."

"But it was only a shadow from the outside, not a shadow coming through from the soul of the girl."

"Yes. you may say so. But it was all that was wanted to make the meaning of her forehead manifest—yes, of her whole face, which had now and then, in the pauses of his passion, perplexed the youth. All of it, curled nostrils, pouting lips, projecting chin, instantly fell into harmony with that darkness between her eyebrows. The youth understood it in a moment, and went home miserable. And they're not married *yet*."

"I caught a toper alone, over his magnum of port," said a very dark Shadow; "and didn't I give it him! I made *delirium tremens* first; and then I settled into a funeral, passing slowly along the length of the opposite wall. I gave him plenty of plumes and mourning coaches. And then I gave him a funeral service, but I could not manage to make the surplice white, which was all the better for such a sinner. The wretch stared till his face passed from purple to grey, and actually left his fifth glass only, unfinished, and took refuge with his wife and children in the drawing-room, much to their surprise. I believe he actually drank a cup of tea; and although I have often looked in since, I have never caught him again, drinking alone at least."

"But does he drink less? Have you done him any good?"

"I hope so; but I am sorry to say I can't feel sure about it."

"Humph! Humph! Humph!" grunted various shadow throats.

"I had such fun once!" cried another. "I made such game of a young clergyman!"

"You have no right to make game of any one."

"Oh yes, I have—when it is for his good. He used to study his sermons—where do you think?"

"In his study, of course. Where else should it be?"

"Yes and no. Guess again."

"Out amongst the faces in the streets?"

"Guess again."

"In still green places in the country?"

"Guess again."

"In old books?"

"Guess again."

"No, no. Tell us."

"In the looking-glass. Ha! ha! ha!"

"He was fair game; fair shadow game."

"I thought so. And I made such fun of him one night on the wall! He had sense enough to see that it was himself, and very like an ape. So he got ashamed, turned the mirror with its face to the wall, and thought a little more about his people, and a little less about himself. I was very glad; for, please your majesty,"—and here the speaker turned towards the king—"we don't like the creatures that live in the mirrors. You call them ghosts, don't you?"

Before the king could reply, another had commenced. But the story about the clergyman had made the king wish to hear one of the shadow-sermons. So he turned him towards a long Shadow, who was preaching to a very quiet and listening crowd. He was just concluding his sermon.

"Therefore, dear Shadows, it is the more needful that we love one another as much as we can, because that is not much. We have no such excuse for not loving as mortals have, for we do not die like them. I suppose it is the thought of that death that makes them hate so much. Then again, we go to sleep all day, most of us, and not in the night, as men do. And you know that we forget everything that happened the night before; therefore, we ought to love well, for the love is short. Ah! dear Shadow, whom I love now with all my shadowy soul, I shall not love thee to-morrow eve, I shall not know thee; I shall pass thee in the crowd and never dream that the Shadow whom I now love is near me then. Happy Shades! for we only remember our tales until we have told them here, and then they vanish in the shadow-churchyard, where we bury only our dead selves. Ah! brethren, who would be a man and remember? Who would be a man and weep? We ought indeed to love one another, for we alone inherit oblivion; we alone are renewed with eternal birth; we alone have no gathered weight of years. I will tell you the awful fate of one Shadow who rebelled against his nature, and sought to remember the past. He said, 'I *will* remember this eve.' He fought with the genial influences of kindly sleep when the sun rose on the awful dead day of light; and although he could not keep quite awake, he dreamed of the foregone eve, and he never forgot his dream. Then he tried again the next night, and the next, and the next; and he tempted another Shadow to try it with him. But at last their awful fate overtook them; for, instead of continuing to be Shadows, they began to cast shadows, as foolish men say; and so they thickened and thickened till they vanished out of our world. They are now condemned to walk the earth a man and a woman, with death behind them, and memories within them. Ah, brother Shades! let us love one another, for we shall soon forget. We are not men, but Shadows."

The king turned away, and pitied the poor Shadows far more than they pitied men.

"Oh! how we played with a musician one night," exclaimed a Shadow in another group, to which the king had first directed a passing thought, and then had stopped to listen.—"Up and down we went, like the hammers and dampers on his piano. But he took his revenge on us. For after he had watched us for half an hour in the twilight, he rose and went to his instrument and played a shadow-dance that fixed us all in sound for ever. Each could tell the very notes meant for him; and as long as he played we could not stop, but went on dancing and dancing after the music, just as the magician—I mean the musician—pleased. And he punished us well; for he nearly danced us all off our legs and out of shape into tired heaps of collapsed and palpitating darkness. We won't go near him for some time again, if we can only remember it. He had been very miserable all day, he was so poor; and we could not think of any way of comforting him except making him laugh. We did not succeed, with our wildest efforts; but it turned out better than we had expected, after all; for his shadow-dance got him into notice, and he is quite popular now, and making money fast.—If he does not take care, we shall have other work to do with him by-and-by, poor fellow!"

"I and some others did the same for a poor play-writer once. He had a Christmas piece to write, and being an original genius, it was not so easy for him to find a subject as it is for most of his class. I saw the trouble he was in, and collecting a few stray Shadows, we acted, in dumb show of course, the funniest bit of nonsense we could think of; and it was quite successful. The poor fellow watched every motion, roaring with laughter at us, and delight at the ideas we put into his head. He turned it all into words, and scenes, and actions; and the piece came off with a splendid success."

"But how long we have to look for a chance of doing anything worth doing!" said a long, thin, especially lugubrious Shadow. "I have only done one thing worth telling ever since we met last. But I am proud of that."

"What was it? What was it?" rose from twenty voices.

"I crept into a dining room, one twilight, soon after Christmas day. I had been drawn thither by the glow of a bright fire shining through red window-curtains. At first I thought there was no one there, and was on the point of leaving the room and going out again into the snowy street, when I suddenly caught the sparkle of eyes. I found that they belonged to a little boy who lay very still on a sofa. I crept into a dark corner by the sideboard, and watched him. He seemed very sad, and did nothing but stare into the fire. At last he

sighed out,—'I wish mamma would come home.'
'Poor boy!' thought I, 'there is no help for that but
mamma.' Yet I would try to while away the time for
him. So out of my corner I stretched a long shadow-
arm, reaching all across the ceiling, and pretended to
make a grab at him. He was rather frightened at first;
but he was a brave boy, and soon saw that it was all
a joke. So when I did it again, he made a clutch at
me; and then we had such fun! For though he often
sighed and wished mamma would come home, he
always began again with me; and on we went with
the wildest game. At last his mother's knock came to
the door, and, starting up in delight, he rushed into
the hall to meet her, and forgot all about poor black
me. But I did not mind that in the least; for when I
glided out after him into the hall, I was well repaid
for my trouble by hearing his mother say to him,—
'Why, Charlie, my dear, you look ever so much better
since I left you!' At that moment I slipped through
the closing door, and as I ran across the snow, I
heard the mother say,—'What Shadow can that be
passing so quickly?' And Charlie answered with a
merry laugh,—'Oh! mamma, I suppose it must be
the funny shadow that has been playing such games
with me all the time you were out.' As soon as the
door was shut, I crept along the wall and looked in
at the dining-room window. And I heard his mamma
say, as she led him into the room,—'What an imagination the boy has!' Ha! ha! ha! Then she looked at
him, and the tears came in her eyes; and she stooped
down over him, and I heard the sounds of a mingling
kiss and sob."

"I always look for nurseries full of children," said
another; and this winter I have been very fortunate.
I am sure children belong especially to us. One evening, looking about in a great city, I saw through the
window into a large nursery, where the odious gas

had not yet been lighted. Round the fire sat a company of the most delightful children I had ever seen.
They were waiting patiently for their tea. It was too
good an opportunity to be lost. I hurried away, and
gathering together twenty of the best Shadows I could
find, returned in a few moments; and entering the
nursery, we danced on the walls one of our best
dances. To be sure it was mostly extemporized; but
I managed to keep it in harmony by singing this song,
which I made as we went on. Of course the children
could not hear it; they only saw the motions that
answered to it; but with them they seemed to be very
much delighted indeed, as I shall presently prove to
you. This was the song: —

'Swing, swang, swingle, swuff!
 Flicker, flacker, fling, fluff!
    Thus we go,
    To and fro;
    Here and there,
    Everywhere,
    Born and bred;
    Never dead,
        Only gone.


    'On! Come on.
    Looming, glooming,
    Spreading, fuming,
    Shattering, scattering,
    Parting, darting,
    Settling, starting,
    All our life
    Is a strife,

*And a wearying for rest*
*On the darkness' friendly breast.*

   *'Joining, splitting,*
   *Rising, sitting,*
   *Laughing, shaking,*
   *Sides all aching,*
*Grumbling, grim, and gruff.*
*Swingle, swangle, swuff!*

   *'Now a knot of darkness;*
     *Now dissolved gloom;*
   *Now a pall of blackness*
     *Hiding all the room.*
*Flicker, flacker, fluff!*
*Black, and black enough!*

   *'Dancing now like demons;*
     *Lying like the dead;*
   *Gladly would we stop it,*
     *And go down to bed!*
*But our work we still must do,*
*Shadow men, as well as you.*

   *'Rooting, rising, shooting,*
     *Heaving, sinking, creeping;*
*Hid in corners crooning;*
     *Splitting, poking, leaping,*
*Gathering, towering, swooning.*
     *When we're lurking,*
     *Yet we're working,*

*For our labour we must do,*
*Shadow men, as well as you.*
  *Flicker, flacker, fling, fluff!*
  *Swing, swang, swingle, swuff!'*

" 'How thick the Shadows are!' said one of the children—a thoughtful little girl.

" 'I wonder where they come from,' said a dreamy little boy.

" 'I think they grow out of the wall,' answered the little girl; 'for I have been watching them come; first one, and then another, and then a whole lot of them. I am sure they grow out of the walls.'

" 'Perhaps they have papas and mammas,' said an older boy, with a smile.

" 'Yes, yes; and the doctor brings them in his pocket,' said another, a consequential little maiden.

" 'No; I'll tell you,' said the older boy: 'they're ghosts.'

" 'But ghosts are white.'

" 'Oh! but these have got black coming down the chimney.'

" 'No,' said a curious-looking, white-faced boy of fourteen, who had been reading by the firelight, and had stopped to hear the little ones talk; 'they're body ghosts; they're not soul ghosts.'

"A silence followed, broken by the first, the dreamy-eyed boy, who said,—

" 'I hope they didn't make me'; at which they all burst out laughing.

"Just then the nurse brought in their tea, and when she proceeded to light the gas we vanished."

"I stopped a murder," cried another.

"How? How? How?"

"I will tell you. I had been lurking about a sick room for some time, where a miser lay, apparently dying. I did not like the place at all, but felt as if I

114

should be wanted there. There were plenty of lurking-places about, for the room was full of all sorts of old furniture, especially cabinets, chests, and presses. I believe he had in that room every bit of the property he had spent a long life in gathering. I found that he had gold and gold in those places; for one night, when his nurse was away, he crept out of bed, mumbling and shaking, and managed to open one of the chests, though he nearly fell down with the effort. I was peeping over his shoulder, and such a gleam of gold fell upon me, that it nearly killed me. But hearing his nurse coming, he slammed the lid down, and I recovered.

"I tried very hard, but I could not do him any good. For although I made all sorts of shapes on the walls and ceiling, representing evil deeds that he had done, of which there were plenty to choose from, I could make no shapes on his brain or conscience. He had no eyes for anything but gold. And it so happened that his nurse had neither eyes nor heart for anything else either.

"One day, as she was seated beside his bed, but where he could not see her, stirring some gruel in a basin, to cool it for him, I saw her take a little phial from her bosom, and I knew by the expression of her face both what it was and what she was going to do with it. Fortunately the cork was a little hard to get out, and this gave me one moment to think.

"The room was so crowded with all sorts of things, that although there were no curtains on the four-post bed to hide from the miser the sight of his precious treasures, there was yet but one small part of the ceiling suitable for casting myself upon in the shape I wished to assume. And this spot was hard to reach. But having discovered that upon this very place lay a dull gleam of firelight thrown from a strange old dusty mirror that stood away in some corner, I got

115

in front of the fire, spied where the mirror was, threw myself upon it, and bounded from its face upon the oval pool of dim light on the ceiling, assuming, as I passed, the shape of an old stooping hag, who poured something from a phial into a basin. I made the handle of the spoon with my own nose, ha! ha!"

And the shadow-hand caressed the shadow-tip of the shadow-nose, before the shadow-tongue resumed.

"The old miser saw me: he would not taste the gruel that night, although his nurse coaxed and scolded till they were both weary. She pretended to taste it herself, and to think it very good; but at last retired into a corner, and after making as if she were eating it, took care to pour it all out into the ashes."

"But she must either succeed, or starve him, at last," interposed a Shadow.

"I will tell you."

"And," interposed another, "he was not worth saving."

"He might repent," suggested a third, who was more benevolent.

"No chance of that," returned the former. "Misers never do. The love of money has less in it to cure itself than any other wickedness into which wretched men can fall. What a mercy it is to be born a Shadow! Wickedness does not stick to us. What do we care for gold!—Rubbish!"

"Amen! Amen! Amen!" came from a hundred shadow-voices.

"You should have let her murder him, and so you would have been quit of him."

"And besides, how was he to escape at last? He could never get rid of her, you know."

"I was going to tell you," resumed the narrator, "only you had so many shadow-remarks to make, that you would not let me."

"Go on; go on."

"There was a little grandchild who used to come and see him sometimes—the only creature the miser cared for. Her mother was his daughter; but the old man would never see her, because she had married against his will. Her husband was now dead, but he had not forgiven her yet. After the shadow he had seen, however, he said to himself, as he lay awake that night—I saw the words on his face—'How shall I get rid of that old devil? If I don't eat I shall die; and if I do eat I shall be poisoned. I wish little Mary would come. Ah! her mother would never have served me so.' He lay awake, thinking such things over and over again, all night long, and I stood watching him from a dark corner, till the dayspring came and shook me out. When I came back next night, the room was tidy and clean. His own daughter, a sad-faced but beautiful woman, sat by his bedside; and little Mary was curled up on the floor by the fire, imitating us, by making queer shadows on the ceiling with her twisted hands. But she could not think however they got there. And no wonder, for I helped her to some very unaccountable ones."

"I have a story about a granddaughter, too," said another, the moment that speaker ceased.

"Tell it. Tell it."

"Last Christmas-day," he began, "I and a troop of us set out in the twilight to find some house where we could all have something to do; for we had made up our minds to act together. We tried several, but found objections to them all. At last we espied a large lonely country-house, and hastening to it, we found great preparations making for the Christmas dinner. We rushed into it, scampered all over it, and made up our minds in a moment that it would do. We amused ourselves in the nursery first, where there were several children being dressed for dinner. We generally do go to the nursery first, your majesty. This time we were especially charmed with a little girl about five years old, who clapped her hands and danced about with delight at the antics we performed; and we said we would do something for her if we had a chance. The company began to arrive; and at every arrival, we rushed to the hall, and cut wonderful capers of wel-come. Between times, we scudded away to see how the dressing went on. One girl about eighteen was delightful. She dressed herself as if she did not care much about it, but could not help doing it prettily. When she took her last look at the phantom in the glass, she half smiled to it. —But *we* do not like those creatures that come into the mirrors at all, your maj-esty. We don't understand them. They are dreadful to us. —She looked rather sad and pale, but very sweet and hopeful. So we wanted to know all about her, and soon found out that she was a distant relation and a great favourite of the gentleman of the house, an old man, in whose face benevolence was mingled with obstinacy and a deep shade of the tyrannical. We could not admire him much; but we would not make up our minds all at once: Shadows never do.

"The dinner-bell rang, and down we hurried. The children all looked happy, and we were merry. But there was one cross fellow among the servants, and didn't we plague him! and didn't we get fun out of him! When he was bringing up dishes, we lay in wait for him at every corner, and sprang upon him from the floor, and from over the banisters, and down from the cornices. He started and stumbled and blundered so in consequence, that his fellow-servants thought he was tipsy. Once he dropped a plate, and had to pick up the pieces, and hurry away with them; and didn't we pursue him as he went! It was lucky for him his master did not see how he went on; but we took care not to let him get into any real scrape, though he was quite dazed with the dodging of the unaccountable shadows. Sometimes he thought the walls were coming down upon him, sometimes that the floor was gaping to swallow him; sometimes that he would be knocked to pieces by the hurrying to and fro, or be smothered in the black crowd.

"When the blazing plum-pudding was carried in, we made a perfect shadow-carnival about it, dancing and mumming in the blue flames, like mad demons. And how the children screamed with delight!

"The old gentleman, who was very fond of children, was laughing his heartiest laugh, when a loud knock came to the hall-door. The fair maiden started, turned paler, and then red as the Christmas fire. I saw it, and flung my hands across her face. She was very glad, and I know she said in her heart, 'You kind Shadow!' which paid me well. Then I followed the rest into the hall, and found there a jolly, handsome, brown-faced sailor, evidently a son of the house. The old man received him with tears in his eyes, and the children with shouts of joy. The maiden escaped in the confusion, just in time to save herself from fainting. We crowded about the lamp to hide her retreat, and nearly put it out; and the butler could not get it to burn up before she had glided into her place again, relieved to find the room so dark. The sailor only had seen her go, and now he sat down beside her, and, without a word, got hold of her hand in the gloom. When we all scattered to the walls and the corners, and the lamp blazed up again, he let her hand go.

"During the rest of the dinner the old man watched the two, and saw that there was something between them, and was very angry. For he was an important man in his own estimation, and they had never consulted him. The fact was, they had never known their own minds till the sailor had gone upon his last voyage, and had learned each other's only this moment. —We found out all this by watching them, and then talking together about it afterwards.—The old gentleman saw, too, that his favourite, who was under such obligation to him for loving her so much, loved his son better than him; and he grew by degrees so jealous that he overshadowed the whole table with his morose looks and short answers. That kind of shadowing is very different from ours; and the Christmas dessert grew so gloomy that we Shadows could not bear it, and were delighted when the ladies rose to go to the drawing-room. The gentlemen would not stay behind the ladies, even for the sake of the well-known wine. So the moody host, notwithstanding his hospitality, was left alone at the table in the great silent room. We followed the company up-stairs to the drawing-room, and thence to the nursery for snap-dragon; but while they were busy with this most shadowy of games, nearly all the Shadows crept downstairs again to the dining-room, where the old man still sat, gnawing the bone of his own selfishness. They crowded into the room, and by using every kind of expansion—blowing themselves out like soap bubbles—they succeeded in heaping up the whole room with shade upon shade. They clustered thickest about the fire and the lamp, till at last they almost drowned them in hills of darkness.

"Before they had accomplished so much, the children, tired with fun and frolic, had been put to bed. But the little girl of five years old, with whom we had been so pleased when first we arrived, could not go to sleep. She had a little room of her own; and I had watched her to bed, and now kept her awake by gambolling in the rays of the night-light. When her eyes were fixed upon me, I took the shape of her grandfather, representing him on the wall as he sat in his chair, with his head bent down and his arms hanging listlessly by his sides. And the child remembered that that was just as she had seen him last; for she had happened to peep in at the dining-room door after all the rest had gone up-stairs. 'What if he should be sitting there still,' thought she, 'all alone in the dark!' She scrambled out of bed and crept down.

"Meantime the others had made the room below so dark, that only the face and white hair of the old man could be dimly discerned in the shadowy crowd. For he had filled his own mind with shadows, which we Shadows wanted to draw out of him. Those shadows are very different from us, your majesty knows. He was thinking of all the disappointments he had had in life, and of all the ingratitude he had met with. And he thought far more of the good he had done, than the good others had got. 'After all I have done for them,' said he, with a sigh of bitterness, 'not one of them cares a straw for me. My own children will be glad when I am gone!'—At that instant he lifted up his eyes and saw, standing close by the door, a tiny figure in a long nightgown. The door behind her was shut. It was my little friend, who had crept in noiselessly. A pang of icy fear shot to the old man's heart, but it melted away as fast, for we made a lane through us for a single ray from the fire to fall on the face of the little sprite; and he thought it was a child of his own that had died when just the age of her child-niece, who now stood looking for her grand-father among the Shadows. He thought she had come out of her grave in the cold darkness to ask why her father was sitting alone on Christmas-day. And he felt he had no answer to give his little ghost, but one he would be ashamed for her to hear. But his grand-child saw him now, and walked up to him with a childish stateliness, stumbling once or twice on what seemed her long shroud. Pushing through the crowded shadows, she reached him, climbed upon his knee, laid her little long-haired head on his shoulders, and said,—'Ganpa! you goomy? Isn't it your Kissy-Day too, ganpa?'

"A new fount of love seemed to burst from the clay of the old man's heart. He clasped the child to his bosom, and wept. Then, without a word, he rose with her in his arms, carried her up to her room, and laying her down in her bed, covered her up, kissed her sweet little mouth unconscious of reproof, and then went to the drawing-room.

"As soon as he entered, he saw the culprits in a quiet corner alone. He went up to them, took a hand of each, and joining them in both his, said, 'God bless you!' Then he turned to the rest of the company, and 'Now,' said he, 'let's have a Christmas carol.'—And well he might; for though I have paid many visits to the house, I have never seen him cross since; and I am sure that must cost him a good deal of trouble."

"We have just come from a great palace," said another, "where we knew there were many children, and where we thought to hear glad voices, and see royally merry looks. But as soon as we entered, we became aware that one mighty Shadow shrouded the whole; and that Shadow deepened and deepened, till it gathered in darkness about the reposing form of a wise prince. When we saw him, we could move no more, but clung heavily to the walls, and by our stillness added to the sorrow of the hour. And when we saw the mother of her people weeping with bowed head for the loss of him in whom she had trusted, we were seized with such a longing to be Shadows no more, but winged angels, which are the white shadows cast in heaven from the Light of Light, so as to gather around her, and hover over her with comforting, that we vanished from the walls, and found ourselves floating high above the towers of the palace, where we met the angels on their way, and knew that our service was not needed."

By this time there was a glimmer of approaching

moonlight, and the king began to see several of those stranger Shadows, with human faces and eyes, moving about amongst the crowd. He knew at once that they did not belong to his dominion. They looked at him, and came near him, and passed slowly, but they never made any obeisance, or gave sign of homage. And what their eyes said to him, the king only could tell. And he did not tell.

"What are those other Shadows that move through the crowd?" said he to one of his subjects near him.

The Shadow started, looked round, shivered slightly, and laid his finger on his lips. Then leading the king a little aside, and looking carefully about him once more,—

"I do not know," said he, in a low tone, "what they are. I have heard of them often, but only once did I ever see any of them before. That was when some of us one night paid a visit to a man who sat much alone, and was said to think a great deal. We saw two of those sitting in the room with him, and he was as pale as they were. We could not cross the threshold, but shivered and shook, and felt ready to melt away. Is not your majesty afraid of them too!"

But the king made no answer; and before he could speak again, the moon had climbed above the mighty pillars of the church of the Shadows, and looked in at the great window of the sky.

The shapes had all vanished; and the king, again lifting up his eyes, saw but the wall of his own chamber, on which flickered the Shadow of a Little Child. He looked down, and there, sitting on a stool by the fire, he saw one of his own little ones, waiting to say good-night to his father, and go to bed early, that he might rise early too, and be very good and happy all Christmas-day.

And Ralph Rinkelmann rejoiced that he was a man, and not a Shadow.

But as the Shadows vanished they left the sense

of song in the king's brain. And the words of their
song must have been something like these: —

*"Shadows, Shadows, Shadows all!*
*Shadow birth and funeral!*
*Shadow moons gleam overhead;*
*Over shadow-graves we tread.*
*Shadow-hope lives, grows, and dies.*

*Shadow-love from shadow-eyes*
*Shadow-ward entices on*
*To shadow-words on shadow-stone,*
*Closing up the shadow-tale*
*With a shadow-shadow-wail.*

*"Shadow-man, thou art a gloom*
*Cast upon a shadow-tomb*
*Through the endless shadow-air,*
*From the Shadow sitting there,*
*On a moveless shadow-throne,*
*Glooming through the ages gone;*
*North and south, and in and out,*
*East and west, and all about,*
*Flinging Shadows everywhere*
*On the shadow-painted air.*
*Shadow-man, thou hast no story;*
*Nothing but a shadow-glory."*

But Ralph Rinkelmann said to himself, —
"They are but Shadows that sing thus; for a Shadow
can see but Shadows. A man sees a man where a
Shadow sees only a Shadow."

And he was comforted in himself.

# THE GIFTS OF THE CHILD CHRIST

## CHAPTER I

"MY hearers, we grow old," said the preacher. "Be it summer or be it spring with us now, autumn will soon settle down into winter, that winter whose snow melts only in the grave. The wind of the world sets for the tomb. Some of us rejoice to be swept along on its swift wings, and hear it bellowing in the hollows of earth and sky; but it will grow a terror to the man of trembling limb and withered brain, until at length he will long for the shelter of the tomb to escape its roaring and buffeting. Happy the man who shall then be able to believe that old age itself, with its pitiable decays and sad dreams of youth, is the chastening of the Lord, a sure sign of his love and his fatherhood."

It was the first Sunday in Advent; but "the chastening of the Lord" came into almost every sermon that man preached.

"Eloquent! But after all, *can* this kind of thing be true?" said to himself a man of about thirty, who sat decorously listening. For many years he had thought he believed this kind of thing—but of late he was not so sure.

Reprinted from *The Gifts of the Child Christ, and Other Tales* (1882).

Beside him sat his wife, in her new winter bonnet, her pretty face turned up toward the preacher; but her eyes—nothing else—revealed that she was not listening. She was much younger than her husband—hardly twenty, indeed.

In the upper corner of the pew sat a pale-faced child about five, sucking her thumb, and staring at the preacher.

The sermon over, they walked home in proximity. The husband looked gloomy, and his eyes sought the ground. The wife looked more smiling than cheerful, and her pretty eyes went hither and thither. Behind them walked the child—steadily, "with level-fronting eyelids."

It was a late-built region of large, commonplace houses, and at one of them they stopped and entered. The door of the dining-room was open, showing the table laid for their Sunday dinner. The gentleman passed on to the library behind it, the lady went up to her bedroom, and the child a stage higher to the nursery.

It wanted half an hour to dinner. Mr. Greatorex sat down, drummed with his fingers on the arm of his easy-chair, took up a book of arctic exploration, threw it again on the table, got up, and went to the smoking-room. He had built it for his wife's sake, but was often glad of it for his own. Again he seated himself, took a cigar, and smoked gloomily.

Having reached her bedroom, Mrs. Greatorex took off her bonnet, and stood for ten minutes turning it round and round. Earnestly she regarded it—now gave a twist to the wire-stem of a flower, then spread wider the loop of a bow. She was meditating what it lacked of perfection rather than brooding over its merits: she was keen in bonnets.

Little Sophy—or, as she called herself by a transposition of consonant sounds common with chil-

dren, Phosy—found her nurse Alice in the nu
But she was lost in the pages of a certain L
weekly, which had found her in a mood open to its
influences, and did not even look up when the child
entered. With some effort Phosy drew off her gloves,
and with more difficulty untied her hat. Then she
took off her jacket, smoothed her hair, and retreated
to a corner. There a large shabby doll lay upon her
little chair: she took it up, disposed it gently upon the
bed, seated herself in its place, got a little book from
where she had left it under the chair, smoothed down
her skirts, and began simultaneously to read and suck
her thumb. The book was an unhealthy one, a cup
filled to the brim with a poverty-stricken and selfish
religion: such are always breaking out like an erup-
tion here and there over the body of the Church, doing
their part, doubtless, in carrying off the evil humours
generated by poverty of blood, or the congestion of
self-preservation. It is wonderful out of what spoiled
fruit some children will suck sweetness.

But she did not read far: her thoughts went back
to a phrase which had haunted her ever since first
she went to church: "Whom the Lord loveth, he
chasteneth."

"I wish he would chasten me," she thought for the
hundredth time.

The small Christian had no suspicion that her
whole life had been a period of chastening—that few
children indeed had to live in such a sunless atmosphere as hers.

Alice threw down the newspaper, gazed from the
window into the back-yard of the next house, saw
nothing but an elderly man-servant brushing a gar-
ment, and turned upon Sophy.

"Why don't you hang up your jacket, miss?" she
said, sharply.

The little one rose, opened the wardrobe-door wide,

carried a chair to it, fetched her jacket from the bed, clambered up on the chair, and leaning far forward to reach a peg, tumbled right into the bottom of the wardrobe.

"You clumsy!" exclaimed the nurse angrily, and pulling her out by the arm, shook her.

Alice was not generally rough to her, but there were reasons to-day.

Phosy crept back to her seat, pale, frightened, and a little hurt. Alice hung up the jacket, closed the wardrobe, and, turning, contemplated her own pretty face and neat figure in the glass opposite. The dinner-bell range.

"There, I declare!" she cried, and wheeled round on Phosy. "And your hair not brushed yet, miss! Will you ever learn to do a thing without being told it? Thank goodness, I shan't be plagued with you long! But I pity her as comes after me: I do!"

"If the Lord would but chasten me!" said the child to herself, as she rose and laid down her book with a sigh.

The maid seized her roughly by the arm, and brushed her hair with an angry haste that made the child's eyes water, and herself feel a little ashamed at the sight of them.

"How could anybody love such a troublesome chit?" she said, seeking the comfort of justification from the child herself.

Another sigh was the poor little damsel's only answer. She looked very white and solemn as she entered the dining-room.

Mr. Greatorex was a merchant in the City. But he was more of a man than a merchant, which all merchants are not. Also, he was more scrupulous in his dealings than some merchants in the same line of business, who yet stood as well with the world as he; but, on the other hand, he had the meanness to pride himself upon it as if it had been something he might have done without and yet held up his head.

Some six years before, he had married to please his parents; and a year before, he had married to please himself. His first wife had intellect, education, and heart, but little individuality—not enough to reflect the individuality of her husband. The consequence was, he found her uninteresting. He was kind and indulgent, however, and not even her best friend blamed him much for manifesting nothing beyond the average devotion of husbands. But in truth his wife had great capabilities, only they had never ripened, and when she died, a fortnight after giving birth to Sophy, her husband had not a suspicion of the large amount of undeveloped power that had passed away with her.

Her child was so like her both in countenance and manner that he was too constantly reminded of her unlamented mother; and he loved neither enough to discover that, in a sense as true as marvellous, the child was the very flower-bud of her mother's nature, in which her retarded blossom had yet a chance of being slowly carried to perfection. Love alone gives insight, and the father took her merely for a miniature edition of the volume which he seemed to have laid aside forever in the dust of the earth's lumber-room. Instead, therefore, of watering the roots of his little human slip from the well of his affections, he had scarcely as yet perceived more in relation to her than that he was legally accountable for her existence, and bound to give her shelter and food. If he had questioned himself on the matter, he would have replied that love was not wanting, only waiting upon her growth, and the development of something to interest him.

Little right as he had had to expect anything from his first marriage, he had yet cherished some hopes therein—tolerably vague, it is true, yet hardly faint enough, it would seem, for he was disappointed in them. When its bonds fell from him, however, he flattered himself that he had not worn them in vain, but had through them arrived at a knowledge of women as rare as profound. But whatever the reach of this knowledge, it was not sufficient to prevent him from harbouring the presumptuous hope of so choosing and so fashioning the heart and mind of a woman that they should be as concave mirrors to his own. I do not mean that he would have admitted the figure, but such was really the end he blindly sought. I wonder how many of those who have been disappointed in such an attempt have been thereby aroused to the perception of what a frightful failure their success would have been on both sides. It was bad enough that Augustus Greatorex's theories had cramped his own development; it would have been ten-fold worse had they been operative to the stunting of another soul.

Letty Merewether was the daughter of a bishop *in partibus*. She had been born tolerably innocent, had grown up more than tolerably pretty, and was, when she came to England at the age of sixteen, as nearly a genuine example of Locke's sheet of white paper as could well have fallen to the hand of such an experimenter as Greatorex would fain become.

In his suit he had prospered—perhaps too easily. He loved the girl, or at least loved the modified reflection of her in his own mind; while she, thoroughly admiring the dignity, good looks, and accomplishments of the man whose attentions flattered her self-opinion, accorded him deference enough to encourage his vainest hopes. Although she knew little, fluttering over the merest surfaces of existence, she had sense enough to know that he talked sense to her, and foolishness enough to put it down to her own credit, while for the sense itself she cared little or nothing. And Greatorex, without even knowing what she was roughhewn for, would take upon him to shape her ends!—an ambition the Divinity never permits to succeed: he who fancies himself the carver finds himself but the chisel, or indeed perhaps only the mallet, in the hand of the true workman.

During the days of his courtship, then, Letty listened and smiled, or answered with what he took for a spiritual response, when it was merely a brain-echo. Looking down into the pond of her being, whose surface was not yet ruffled by any bubbling of springs from below, he saw the reflection of himself and was satisfied. An able man on his hobby looks a centaur of wisdom and folly; but if he be at all a wise man, the beast will one day or other show him the jade's favour of unseating him. Meantime Augustus Greatorex was fooled, not by poor little Letty, who was not capable of fooling him, but by himself. Letty had made no pretences; had been interested, and had shown her interest; had understood, or seemed to understand, what he said to her, and forgotten it the next moment—had no pocket to put it in, did not know what to do with it, and let it drop into the Limbo of Vanity. They had not been married many days before the scouts of advancing disappointment were upon them. Augustus resisted manfully for a time. But the truth was each of the two had to become a great deal more than either was, before any approach to unity was possible. He tried to interest her in one subject after another—tried her first, I am ashamed to say, with political economy. In that instance, when he came home to dinner he found that she had not got beyond the first page of the book he had left with her. But she had the best of excuses, namely, that of that page she had not understood a sentence. He saw his mistake, and tried her with poetry. But Milton, with whom unfortunately he commenced his approaches, was to her, if not equally unintelligible, equally uninteresting. He tried her next with the elements of science, but with no better success. He returned to poetry, and read some of the *Faerie Queene* with her: she was, or seemed to be, interested in all his talk about it, and inclined to go on with it in his absence, but found the first stanza she tried more than enough without him to give life to it. She could give it none, and therefore it gave her none. I believe she read a chapter of the Bible every day, but the only books she read with any real interest were novels of a sort that Augustus despised. It never occurred to him that he ought at once to have made friends of this Momus of unrighteousness, for by it he might have found entrance to the sealed chamber. He ought to have read with her the books she did like, for by them only could he make her think, and from them alone could he lead her to better. It is but from the very step upon which one stands that one can move to the next. Besides these books, there was nothing in her scheme of the universe but fashion, dress, calls, the park, other-peopledom, concerts, plays, church-going—whatever could show itself on the frosted glass of her *camera obscura*—make an interest of motion and colour in her darkened chamber. Without these, her bosom's mistress would have found life unendurable, for not yet had she ascended her throne, but lay on the floor of her nursery, surrounded with toys that imitated life.

It was no wonder, therefore, that Augustus was at length compelled to allow himself disappointed. That it was the fault of his self-confidence made the thing no whit better. He was too much of a man not to cherish a certain tenderness for her, but he soon found to his dismay that it had begun to be mingled with a shadow of contempt. Against this he struggled, but with fluctuating success. He stopped later and later at business, and when he came home spent more and more of his time in the smoking-room, where by and by he had bookshelves put up. Occasionally he would accept an invitation to dinner and accompany his wife, but he detested evening parties, and when Letty, who never refused an invitation if she could help it, went to one, he remained at home with his books. But his power of reading began to diminish. He became restless and irritable. Something kept gnawing at his heart. There was a sore spot in it. The spot grew larger and larger, and by degrees the centre of his consciousness came to be a soreness: his cherished idea had been fooled; he had taken a silly girl for a woman of undeveloped wealth; —a bubble, a surface whereon fair colours chased each other, for a hearted crystal.

On her part, Letty too had her grief, which, unlike Augustus, she did not keep to herself, receiving in return from more than one of her friends the soothing assurance that Augustus was only like all other men; that women were but their toys, which they cast away when weary of them. Letty did not see that she was herself making a toy of her life, or that Augustus was right in refusing to play with such a costly and delicate thing. Neither did Augustus see that, having, by his own blunder, married a mere child, he was bound to deal with her as one, and not let the child suffer for his fault more than what could not be helped. It is not by pressing our insights upon them, but by bathing the sealed eyelids of the human kittens, that we can help them.

And all the time poor little Phosy was left to the care of Alice, a clever, careless, good-hearted, self-satisfied damsel, who, although seldom so rough in her behaviour as we have just seen her, abandoned the child almost entirely to her own resources. It was often she sat alone in the nursery, wishing the Lord would chasten her—because then he would love her.

The first course was nearly over ere Augustus had brought himself to ask—

"What did you think of the sermon today, Letty?"

"Not much," answered Letty. "I am not fond of finery. I prefer simplicity."

Augustus held his peace bitterly. For it was just finery in a sermon, without knowing it, that Letty was fond of: what seemed to him a flimsy syllabub of sacred things, beaten up with the whisk of composition, was charming to Letty; while, on the contrary, if a man such as they had been listening to was carried away by the thoughts that struggled in him for utterance, the result, to her judgment, was finery, and the object display. In excuse it must be remembered that she had been used to her father's style, which no one could have aspersed with lack of sobriety.

Presently she spoke again.

"Gus, dear, couldn't you make up your mind for once to go with me to Lady Ashdaile's to-morrow? I am getting quite ashamed of appearing so often without you."

"There is another way of avoiding that unpleasantness," remarked her husband drily.

"You cruel creature!" returned Letty playfully. "But I must go this once, for I promised Mrs. Holden."

"You know, Letty," said her husband, after a little pause, "it gets of more and more consequence that you should not fatigue yourself. By keeping such late hours in such stifling rooms you are endangering two lives—remember that, Letty. If you stay at home to-morrow, I will come home early, and read to you all the evening."

"Gussy, that *would* be charming. You *know* there

is nothing in the world I should enjoy so much. But this time I really mustn't."

She launched into a list of all the great nobodies and small somebodies who were to be there, and whom she positively must see: it might be her only chance.

Those last words quenched a sarcasm on Augustus' lips. He was kinder than usual the rest of the evening, and read her to sleep with the Pilgrim's Progress.

Phosy sat in a corner, listened, and understood. Or where she misunderstood, it was an honest misunderstanding, which never does much hurt. Neither father nor mother spoke to her till they bade her good night. Neither saw the hungry heart under the mask of the still face. The father never imagined her already fit for the modelling she was better without, and the stepmother had to become a mother before she could value her.

Phosy went to bed to dream of the Valley of Humiliation.

## CHAPTER II

THE next morning Alice gave her mistress warning. It was quite unexpected, and she looked at her aghast.

"Alice," she said at length, "you're never going to leave me at such a time!"

"I'm sorry it don't suit you, ma'am, but I must."

"Why, Alice? What is the matter? Has Sophy been troublesome?"

"No, ma'am; there's no harm in that child."

"Then what can it be, Alice? Perhaps you are going to be married sooner than you expected?"

Alice gave her chin a little toss, pressed her lips together, and was silent.

"I have always been kind to you," resumed her mistress.

"I'm sure, ma'am, I never made no complaints!" returned Alice, but as she spoke she drew herself up straighter than before.

"Then what is it?" said her mistress.

"The fact is, ma'am," answered the girl, almost fiercely, "I can*not* any longer endure a state of domestic slavery."

"I don't understand you a bit better," said Mrs. Greatorex, trying, but in vain, to smile, and therefore looking angrier than she was.

"I mean, ma'am—an' I see no reason as I shouldn't say it, for it's the truth—there's a worm at the root of society where one yuman bein' 's got to do the dirty work of another. I don't mind sweepin' up my own dust, but I won't sweep up nobody else's. I ain't a goin' to demean myself no longer! There!"

"Leave the room, Alice," said Mrs. Greatorex; and when, with a toss and a flounce, the young woman had vanished, she burst into tears of anger and annoyance.

The day passed. The evening came. She dressed without Alice's usual help, and went to Lady Ashdaile's with her friend. There a reaction took place, and her spirits rose unnaturally. She even danced—to the disgust of one or two quick-eyed matrons who sat by the wall.

When she came home she found her husband sitting up for her. He said next to nothing, and sat up an hour longer with his book.

In the night she was taken ill. Her husband called Alice, and ran himself to fetch the doctor. For some hours she seemed in danger, but by noon was much better. Only the greatest care was necessary.

As soon as she could speak, she told Augustus of Alice's warning, and he sent for her to the library.

She stood before him with flushed cheeks and flashing eyes.

"I understand, Alice, you have given your mistress warning," he said gently.

"Yes, sir."

"Your mistress is very ill, Alice."

"Yes, sir."

"Don't you think it would be ungrateful of you to leave her in her present condition? She's not likely to be strong for some time to come."

The use of the word "ungrateful" was an unfortunate one. Alice begged to know what she had to be grateful for. Was her work worth nothing? And her master, as every one must who claims that which can only be freely given, found himself in the wrong.

"Well, Alice," he said, "we won't dispute that point; and if you are really determined on going, you must do the best you can for your mistress for the rest of the month."

Alice's sense of injury was soothed by her master's forbearance. She had always rather approved of Mr. Greatorex, and she left the room more softly than she had entered it.

Letty had a fortnight in bed, during which she reflected a little.

The very next day on which she left her room, Alice sought an interview with her master, and declared she could not stay out her month; she must go home at once.

She had been very attentive to her mistress during the fortnight: there must be something to account for her strange behaviour.

"Come now, Alice," said her master, "what's at the back of all this? You have been a good, well-behaved, obliging girl till now, and I am certain you would never be like this if there weren't something wrong somewhere."

"Something wrong, sir! No, indeed, sir! Except you call it wrong to have an old uncle as dies and leaves ever so much money—thousands on thousands, the lawyers say."

"And does it come to you then, Alice?"

"I get my share, sir. He left it to be parted even between his nephews and nieces."

"Why, Alice, you are quite an heiress, then!" returned her master, scarcely, however, believing the thing so grand as Alice would have it. "But don't you think now it would be rather hard that your fortune should be Mrs. Greatorex's misfortune?"

"Well, I don't see as how it shouldn't," replied Alice. "It's mis'ess's fortun' as 'as been my misfortun'—ain't it now, sir? An' why shouldn't it be the other way next?"

"I don't quite see how your mistress's fortune can be said to be your misfortune, Alice."

"Anybody would see that, sir, as wasn't blinded by class-prejudices."

"Class-prejudices!" exclaimed Mr. Greatorex, in surprise at the word.

"It's a term they use, I believe, sir! But it's plain enough that if mis'ess hadn't 'a' been better off than me, she wouldn't ha' been able to secure my services—as you calls it."

"That is certainly plain enough," returned Mr. Greatorex. "But suppose nobody had been able to secure your services, what would have become of you?"

"By that time the people'd have rose to assert their rights."

"To what?—To fortunes like yours?"

"To bread and cheese at least, sir," returned Alice, pertly.

"Well, but you've had something better than bread and cheese."

"I don't make no complaints as to the style of livin'
in the house, sir, but that's all one, so long as it's on
the vile condition of domestic slavery—which it's
nothing can justify."

"Then of course, although you are now a woman
of property, you will never dream of having any one
to wait on you," said her master, amused with the
volume of human nature thus opened to him.

"All I say, sir, is—it's my turn now; and I ain't
goin' to be sit upon by no one. I know my dooty to
myself."

"I didn't know there was such a duty, Alice," said
her master.

Something in his tone displeased her.

"Then you know now, sir," she said, and bounced
out of the room.

The next moment, however, ashamed of her rudeness, she re-entered, saying,

"I don't want to be unkind, sir, but I must go home.
I've got a brother that's ill, too, and wants to see me.
If you don't object to me goin' home for a month, I
promise you to come back and see mis'ess through
her trouble—as a friend, you know, sir."

"But just listen to me first, Alice," said Mr. Greatorex. "I've had something to do with wills in my
time, and I can assure you it is not likely to be less
than a year before you can touch the money. You had
much better stay where you are till your uncle's af-
fairs are settled. You don't know what may happen.
There's many a slip between cup and lip, you know."

"Oh! it's all right, sir. Everybody knows the money's
left to his nephews and nieces, and me and my
brother's as good as any."

"I don't doubt it: still, if you'll take my advice, you'll
keep a sound roof over your head till another's ready
for you."

Alice only threw her chin in the air, and said almost threateningly,

"Am I to go for the month, sir?"

"I'll talk to your mistress about it," answered Mr. Greatorex, not at all sure that such an arrangement would be for his wife's comfort.

But the next day Mrs. Greatorex had a long talk with Alice, and the result was that on the following Monday she was to go home for a month, and then return for two months more at least. What Mr. Greatorex had said about the legacy, had had its effect, and, besides, her mistress had spoken to her with pleasure in her good fortune. About Sophy no one felt any anxiety: she was no trouble to any one, and the housemaid would see to her.

## CHAPTER III

ON the Sunday evening, Alice's lover, having heard, not from herself, but by a side wind, that she was going home the next day, made his appearance in Wimborne Square, somewhat perplexed—both at the move, and at her leaving him in ignorance of the same. He was a cabinet-maker in an honest shop in the neighbourhood, and in education, faculty, and general worth, considerably Alice's superior,—a fact which had hitherto rather pleased her, but now gave zest to the change which she imagined had subverted their former relation. Full of the sense of her new superiority, she met him draped in an indescribable strangeness. John Jephson felt, at the very first word, as if her voice came from the other side of the English Channel. He wondered what he had done, or rather what Alice could imagine he had done or said, to put her in such tantrums.

"Alice, my dear," he said—for John was a man to go straight at the enemy, "what's amiss? What's come over you? You ain't altogether like your own self to-night! And here I find you're goin' away, and ne'er a word to me about it! What have I done?"

Alice's chin alone made reply. She waited the fitting moment, with splendour to astonish, and with grandeur to subdue her lover. To tell the sad truth, she was no longer sure that it would be well to encourage him on the old footing; was she not standing on tiptoe, her skirts in her hand, on the brink of the brook that parted serfdom from gentility, on the point of stepping daintily across, and leaving domestic slavery, red hands, caps, and obedience behind her? How then was she to marry a man that had black nails, and smelt of glue? It was incumbent on her at least, for propriety's sake, to render him at once aware that it was in condescension ineffable she took any notice of him.

"Alice, my girl!" began John again, in expostulatory tone.

"Miss Cox, if you please, John Jephson," interposed Alice.

"What on 'arth's come over you?" exclaimed John, with the first throb of rousing indignation. "But if you ain't your own self no more, why, Miss Cox be it. 'T seems to me's if I warn't my own self no more—'s if I'd got into some un else, or 't least hedn't got my own ears on m' own head. —Never saw or heerd Alice like this afore!" he added, turning in gloomy bewilderment to the housemaid for a word of human sympathy.

The movement did not altogether please Alice, and she felt she must justify her behaviour.

"You see, John," she said, with dignity, keeping her back towards him, and pretending to dust the globe of a lamp, "there's things as no woman can help, and therefore as no man has no right to complain of them. It's not as if I'd gone an' done it, or

changed myself, no more 'n if it 'ad took place in my
cradle. What can I help it, if the world goes and
changes itself? Am I to blame?—tell me that. It's not
that I make no complaint, but I tell you it ain't me,
it's circumstances as is gone and changed their-
selves, and bein' as circumstances is changed, things
ain't the same as they was, and Miss is the properer
term from you to me, John Jephson."

"Dang it if I know what you're a drivin' at, Alice!—
Miss Cox!—and I beg yer perdon, miss, I'm sure.—
Dang me if I do!"

"Don't swear, John Jephson—leastways before a
lady. It's not proper."

"It seems to me, Miss Cox, as if the wind was a
settin' from Bedlam, or maybe Colney Hatch," said
John, who was considered a humourist among his
comrades. "I wouldn't take no liberties with a lady,
Miss Cox; but if I might be so bold as to arst the joke
of the thing—"

"Joke, indeed!" cried Alice. "Do you call a dead
uncle and ten thousand pounds a joke?"

"God bless me!" said John. "You don't mean it,
Alice?"

"I do mean it, and that you'll find, John Jephson.
I'm goin' to bid you good-bye tomorrer."

"Whoy, Alice!" exlaimed honest John, aghast.

"It's truth I tell ye," said Alice.

"And for how long?" gasped John, forefeeling illim-
itable misfortune.

"That depends," returned Alice, who did not care
to lessen the effect of her communication by men-
tioning her promised return for a season. "— It ain't
likely," she added, "as a heiress is a goin' to act the
nuss-maid much longer."

"But Alice," said John, "you don't mean to say—
it's not in your mind now—it can't be, Alice—you're
only jokin' with me—"

"Indeed, and I'm not!" interjected Alice, with a sniff.

"I don't mean that way, you know. What I mean is, you don't mean as how this 'ere money—dang it all!—as how it's to be all over between you and me?—You *can't* mean that, Alice!" ended the poor fellow, with a choking in his throat.

It was very hard upon him! He must either look as if he wanted to share her money, or else as if he were ready to give her up.

"Arst yourself, John Jephson," answered Alice, "whether it's likely a young lady of fortun' would be keepin' company with a young man as didn't know how to take off his hat to her in the park?"

Alice did not above half mean what she said: she wished mainly to enhance her own importance. At the same time she did mean it half, and that would have been enough for Jephson. He rose, grievously wounded.

"Good-bye, Alice," he said, taking the hand she did not refuse. "Ye're throwin' from ye what all yer money won't buy."

She gave a scornful little laugh, and John walked out of the kitchen.

At the door he turned with one lingering look; but in Alice there was no sign of softening. She turned scornfully away, and no doubt enjoyed her triumph to the full.

The next morning she went away.

## CHAPTER IV

**M**R. Greatorex had ceased to regard the advent of Christmas with much interest. Naturally gifted with a strong religious tendency, he had, since his first marriage, taken, not to denial, but to the side of objection, spending much energy in contempt for the foolish opinions of others, a self-indulgence which does less than little to further the growth of one's own spirit in truth and righteousness. The only person who stands excused—I do not say justified—in so doing, is the man who, having been taught the same opinions, has found them a legion of adversaries barring his way to the truth. But having got rid of them for himself, it is, I suspect, worse than useless to attack them again, save as the ally of those who are fighting their way through the same ranks to the truth. Greatorex had been indulging his intellect at the expense of his heart. A man may have light in the brain and darkness in the heart. It were better to be an owl than a strong-eyed apteryx. He was on the path which naturally ends in blindness and unbelief. I fancy, if he had not been neglectful of his child, she would ere this time have relighted his Christmas-candles for him; but now his second disappointment in marriage had so dulled his heart that he had begun to regard life as a stupid affair, in which the most enviable fool was the man who could still expect to realize an ideal. He had set out on a false track altogether, but had not yet discovered that there had been an immoral element at work in his mistake.

For what right had he to desire the fashioning of any woman after his ideas? Did not the angel of her eternal Ideal for ever behold the face of her Father in heaven? The best that can be said for him is, that, notwithstanding his disappointment and her faults, yea, notwithstanding his own faults, which were, with all his cultivation and strength of character, yet more serious than hers, he was still kind to her; yes, I may say for him, notwithstanding even her silliness, which is a sickening fault, and one which no supremacy of beauty can overshadow, he still loved her a little. Hence the care he showed for her in respect of the coming sorrow was genuine; it did not all belong to his desire for a son to whom he might be a father indeed—after his own fancies, however. Letty, on her part, was as full of expectation as the girl who has been promised a doll that can shut and open its eyes, and cry when it is pinched; her carelessness of its safe arrival came of ignorance and not indifference.

It cannot but seem strange that such a man should have been so careless of the child he had. But from the first she had painfully reminded him of her mother, with whom in truth he had never quarrelled, but with whom he had not found life the less irksome on that account. Add to this that he had been growing fonder of business,—a fact which indicated, in a man of his endowment and development, an inclination downwards of the plane of his life. It was some time since he had given up reading poetry. History had almost followed: he now read little except politics, travels, and popular expositions of scientific progress.

That year Christmas Eve fell upon a Monday. The day before, Letty not feeling very well, her husband thought it better not to leave her, and gave up going to church. Phosy was utterly forgotten, but she dressed herself, and at the usual hour appeared with her prayer-book in her hand ready for church. When her father told her that he was not going, she looked so blank that he took pity upon her, and accompanied her to the church-door, promising to meet her as she came out. Phosy sighed from relief as she entered, for she had a vague idea that by going to church to pray for it she might move the Lord to chasten her. At least he would see her there, and might think of it. She had never had such an attention from her father before, never such dignity conferred upon her as to be allowed to appear in church alone, sitting in the pew by herself like a grown damsel. But I doubt if there was any pride in her stately step, or any vanity in the smile—no, not smile, but illuminated mist, the

vapour of smiles, which haunted her sweet little solemn church-window of a face, as she walked up the
aisle.

The preacher was one of whom she had never heard
her father speak slighting word, in whom her un-
bounded trust had never been shaken. Also he was
one who believed with his whole soul in the things
that make Christmas precious. To him the birth of
the wonderful baby hinted at hundreds of strange
things in the economy of the planet. That a man could
so thoroughly persuade himself that he believed the
old fable, was matter of marvel to some of his friends
who held blind Nature the eternal mother, and Night
the everlasting grandmother of all things. But the
child Phosy, in her dreams or out of them, in church
or nursery, with her book or her doll, was never out
of the region of wonders, and would have believed,
or tried to believe, anything that did not involve a
moral impossibility.

What the preacher said I need not even partially
repeat; it is enough to mention a certain metamor-
phosed deposit from the stream of his eloquence carried home in her mind by Phosy: from some of his
sayings about the birth of Jesus into the world, into
the family, into the individual human bosom, she had
got it into her head that Christmas Day was not a
birthday like that she had herself last year, but that,
in some wonderful way, to her requiring no expla-
nation, the baby Jesus was born every Christmas
Day afresh. What became of him afterwards she did
not know, and indeed she had never yet thought to
ask how it was that he could come to every house in
London as well as No. 1, Wimborne Square. Little of
a home as another might think it, that house was yet
to her the centre of all houses, and the wonder had
not yet widened rippling beyond it: into that spot of
the pool the eternal gift would fall.

Her father forgot the time over his book, but so entranced was her heart with the expectation of the promised visit, now so near—the day after to-morrow—that, if she did not altogether forget to look for him as she stepped down the stair from the church door to the street, his absence caused her no uneasiness; and when, just as she reached it, he opened the house-door in tardy haste to redeem his promise, she looked up at him with a solemn, smileless repose, born of spiritual tension and speechless anticipation, upon her face, and walking past him without change in the rhythm of her motion, marched stately up the stairs to the nursery. I believe the centre of her hope was that when the baby came she would beg him on her knees to ask the Lord to chasten her.

When dessert was over, her mother on the sofa in the drawing-room, and her father in an easy-chair, with a bottle of his favourite wine by his side, she crept out of the room and away again to the nursery. There she reached up to her little bookshelf, and, full of the sermon as spongy mists are full of the sunlight, took thence a volume of stories from the German, the re-reading of one of which, narrating the visit of the Christ-child, laden with gifts, to a certain household, and what he gave to each and all therein, she had, although sorely tempted, saved up until now and sat down with it by the fire, the only light she had. When the housemaid, suddenly remembering she must put her to bed, and at the same time discovering it was a whole hour past her usual time, hurried to the nursery, she found her fast asleep in her little arm-chair, her book on her lap, and the fire self-consumed into a dark cave with a sombre glow in its deepest hollows. Dreams had doubtless come to deepen the impressions of sermon and *mährchen*, for as she slowly yielded to the hands of Polly putting her to bed, her lips, unconsciously moved of the

147

slumbering but not sleeping spirit, more than once murmured the words *Lord loveth and chasteneth*. Right blessedly would I enter the dreams of such a child— revel in them, as a bee in the heavenly gulf of a cactus-flower.

## CHAPTER V

ON Christmas Eve the church bells were ringing through the murky air of London, whose streets lay flaring and steaming below. The brightest of their constellations were the butchers' shops, with their shows of prize beef; around them, the eddies of the human tides were most confused and knotted. But the toy-shops were brilliant also. To Phosy they would have been the treasure-caves of the Christ-child—all mysteries, all with insides to them—boxes, and desks, and windmills, and dove-cots, and hens with chickens, and who could tell what all? In every one of those shops her eyes would have searched for the Christ-child, the giver of all their wealth. For to her he was everywhere that night—ubiquitous as the luminous mist that brooded all over London—of which, however, she saw nothing but the glow above the mews. John Jephson was out in the middle of all the show, drifting about in it: he saw nothing that had pleasure in it, his heart was so heavy. He never thought once of the Christ-child, or even of the Christ-man, as the giver of anything. Birth is the one standing promise-hope for the race, but for poor John this Christmas held no promise. With all his humour, he was one of those people, generally dull and slow— God grant me and mine such dulness and such sloth—who having once loved, cannot cease. During the fortnight he had scarce had a moment's ease from the sting of his Alice's treatment. The honest fellow's feelings were no study to himself; he knew nothing but the pleasure and the pain of them; but I believe it was not mainly for himself that he was sorry. Like Othello, "the pity of it" haunted him: he had taken Alice for a downright girl, about whom there was and could be no mistake; and the first hot blast of prosperity had swept her away like a hectic leaf. What were all the shops dressed out in holly and mistletoe, what were all the rushing flaming gas-jets, what the fattest of prize-pigs to John, who could never more imagine a spare-rib on the table between Alice and him of a Sunday? His imagination ran on seeing her pass in her carriage, and drop him a nod of condescension as she swept noisily by him—trudging home weary from his work to his loveless fireside. *He* didn't want her money! Honestly, he would rather have her without than with money, for he now regarded it as an enemy, seeing what evil changes it could work. "There be some devil in it, sure!" he said to himself. True, he had never found any in his week's wages, but he did remember once finding the devil in a month's wages received in the lump.

As he was thus thinking with himself, a carriage came suddenly from a side street into the crowd, and while he stared at it, thinking Alice might be sitting inside it while he was tramping the pavement alone, she passed him on the other side on foot—was actually pushed against him: he looked round, and saw a young woman, carrying a small bag, disappearing in the crowd. "There's an air of Alice about *her*," said John to himself, seeing her back only. But of course it couldn't be Alice; for her he must look in the carriages now! And what a fool he was: every young woman reminded him of the one he had lost! Perhaps if he was to call the next day—Polly was a good-natured creature—he might hear some news of her.

It had been a troubled fortnight with Mrs. Greatorex. She wished much that she could have talked

to her husband more freely, but she had not learned
to feel at home with him. Yet he had been kinder and
more attentive than usual all the time, so much so
that Letty thought with herself—if she gave him a
boy, he would certainly return to his first devotion.
She said *boy*, because any one might see he cared
little for Phosy. She had never discovered that he was
disappointed in herself, but, since her disregard of
his wishes had brought evil upon her, she had begun
to suspect that he had some ground for being dissat-
isfied with her. She never dreamed of his kindness as
the effort of a conscientious nature to make the best
of what could not now be otherwise helped. Her own
poverty of spirit and lack of worth achieved, she knew
as little of as she did of the riches of Michael the
archangel. One must have begun to gather wisdom
before he can see his own folly.

That evening she was seated alone in the drawing-
room, her husband having left her to smoke his cigar,
when the butler entered and informed her that Alice
had returned, but was behaving so oddly that they
did not know what to do with her. Asking wherein
her oddness consisted, and learning that it was mostly
in silence and tears, she was not sorry to gather that
some disappointment had befallen her, and felt con-
siderable curiosity to know what it was. She therefore
told him to send her upstairs.

Meantime Polly, the housemaid, seeing plainly
enough from her return in the middle of her holiday,
and from her utter dejection, that Alice's expectations
had been frustrated, and cherishing no little resent-
ment against her because of her *uppishness* on the
first news of her good fortune, had been ungenerous
enough to take her revenge in a way as stinging in
effect as bitter in intention; for she loudly protested
that no amount of such luck as she pretended to suppose in Alice's possession, would have induced *her*

to behave herself so that a handsome, honest fellow like John Jephson should be driven to despise her, and take up with her betters. When her mistress's message came, Alice was only too glad to find refuge from the kitchen in the drawing-room.

The moment she entered, she fell on her knees at the foot of the couch on which her mistress lay, covered her face with her hands, and sobbed grievously.

Nor was the change more remarkable in her bearing than in her person. She was pale and worn, and had a hunted look—was in fact a mere shadow of what she had been. For a time her mistress found it impossible to quiet her so as to draw from her her story: tears and sobs combined with repugnance to hold her silent.

"Oh, ma'am!" she burst out at length, wringing her hands, "how ever *can* I tell you? You will never speak to me again. Little did I think such a disgrace was waiting me!"

"It was no fault of yours if you were misinformed," said her mistress, "or that your uncle was not the rich man you fancied."

"Oh, ma'am, there was no mistake there! He was more than twice as rich as I fancied. If he had only died a beggar, and left things as they was!"

"Then he didn't leave it to his nephews and nieces as they told you?—Well, there's no disgrace in that."

"Oh! but he did, ma'am: that was all right; no mistake there either, ma'am.—And to think o' me behavin' as I did—to you and master as was so good to me! Who'll ever take any more notice of me now, after what has come out—as I'm sure I no more dreamed on than the child unborn!"

An agonized burst of fresh weeping followed, and it was with prolonged difficulty, and by incessant questioning, that Mrs. Greatorex at length drew from her the following facts.

Before Alice and her brother could receive the legacy to which they laid claim, it was necessary to produce certain documents, the absence of which, as of any proof to take their place, led to the unavoidable publication of a fact previously known only to a living few—namely, that the father and mother of Alice Hopwood had never been married, which fact deprived them of the smallest claim on the legacy, and fell like a millstone upon Alice and her pride. From the height of her miserable arrogance she fell prone— not merely hurled back into the lowly condition from which she had raised her head only to despise it with base unrighteousness, and to adopt and reassert the principles she had abhorred when they affected herself—not merely this, but, in her own judgment at least, no longer the respectable member of society she had hitherto been justified in supposing herself. The relation of her father and mother she felt overshadow her with a disgrace unfathomable—the more overwhelming that it cast her from the gates of the Paradise she had seemed on the point of entering: her fall she measured by the height of the social ambition she had cherished, and had seemed on the point of attaining. But it is not an evil that the devil's money, which this legacy had from the first proved to Alice, should turn to a hot cinder in the hand. Rarely had a more haughty spirit than hers gone before a fall, and rarely has the fall been more sudden or more abject. And the consciousness of the behaviour into which her false riches had seduced her, changed the whip of her chastisement into scorpions. Worst of all, she had insulted her lover as beneath her notice, and the next moment had found herself too vile for his. Judging by herself, in the injustice of bitter humiliation she imagined him scoffing with his mates at the base-born menial who would set up for a fine lady. But had she been more worthy of honest

John, she would have understood him better. As it was, no really good fortune could have befallen her but such as now seemed to her the depth of evil fortune. Without humiliation to prepare the way for humility, she must have become capable of more and more baseness, until she lost all that makes life worth having.

When Mrs. Greatorex had given her what consolation she found handy, and at length dismissed her, the girl, unable to endure her own company, sought the nursery, where she caught Phosy in her arms and embraced her with fervour. Never in her life having been the object of any such display of feeling, Phosy was much astonished: when Alice had set her down and she had resumed her seat by the fireside, she went on staring for a while—and then a strange sort of miming ensued.

It was Phosy's habit—one less rare with children than may by most be imagined—to do what she could to enter into any state of mind whose shows were sufficiently marked for her observation. She sought to lay hold of the feeling that produced the expression: less than the reproduction of a similar condition in her own imaginative sensorium, subject to her leisurely examination, would in no case satisfy the little metaphysician. But what was indeed very odd was the means she took for arriving at the sympathetic knowledge she desired. As if she had been the most earnest student of dramatic expression through the facial muscles, she would sit watching the countenance of the object of her solicitude, all the time, with full consciousness, fashioning her own as nearly as she could into the lines and forms of the other: in proportion as she succeeded, the small psychologist imagined she felt in herself the condition that produced the phenomenon she observed—as if the shape of her face cast inward its shadow upon her mind, and so revealed to it, through the two faces, what was moving and shaping in the mind of the other.

In the present instance, having at length, after modelling and remodelling her face like that of a gutta-percha doll for some time, composed it finally into the best correspondence she could effect, she sat brooding for a while, with Alice's expression as it were frozen upon it. Gradually the forms assumed melted away, and allowed her still, solemn face to look out from behind them. The moment this evanishment was complete, she rose and went to Alice, where she sat staring into the fire, unconscious of the scrutiny she had been undergoing, and looking up in her face, took her thumb out of her mouth, and said,

"Is the Lord chastening Alice? I wish he would chasten Phosy."

Her face as calm as that of the Sphinx; there was no mist in the depth of her gray eyes, not a cloud on the wide heaven of her forehead.

Was the child crazed? What could the atom mean, with her big eyes looking right into her? Alice never had understood her: it were indeed strange if the less should comprehend the greater! She was not yet capable of recognising the word of the Lord in the mouth of babes and sucklings. But there was a something in Phosy's face besides its calmness and unintelligibility. What it was Alice could never have told—yet it did her good. She lifted the child on her lap. There she soon fell asleep. Alice undressed her, laid her in her crib, and went to bed herself.

But, weary as she was, she had to rise again before she got to sleep. Her mistress was again taken ill. Doctor and nurse were sent for in hot haste; hansom cabs came and went throughout the night, like noisy moths to the one lighted house in the street; there were soft steps within, and doors were gently opened

Her face as calm as that of the Sphinx;
there was no mist in the depth of her gray eyes,
not a cloud on the wide heaven of her forehead.

and shut. The waters of Mara had risen and filled the house.

Towards morning they were ebbing slowly away. Letty did not know that her husband was watching by her bedside. The street was quiet now. So was the house. Most of its people had been up throughout the night, but now they had all gone to bed except the strange nurse and Mr. Greatorex.

It was the morning of Christmas Day, and little Phosy knew it in every cranny of her soul. She was not of those who had been up all night, and now she was awake, early and wide, and the moment she awoke she was speculating: He was coming to-day— *how* would he come? Where should she find the baby Jesus? And when would he come? In the morning, or the afternoon, or in the evening? Could such a grief be in store for her as that he would not appear until night, when she would be again in bed? But she would not sleep till all hope was gone. Would everybody be gathered to meet him, or would he show himself to one after another, each alone? Then her turn would be last, and oh, if he would not come to the nursery! But perhaps he would not appear to her at all!—for was she not one whom the Lord did not care to chasten?

Expectation grew and wrought in her until she could lie in bed no longer. Alice was fast asleep. It must be early, but whether it was yet light or not she could not tell for the curtains. Anyhow she would get up and dress, and then she would be ready for Jesus whenever he should come. True, she was not able to dress herself very well, but he would know, and would not mind. She made all the haste she could, consistently with taking pains, and was soon attired after a fashion.

She crept out of the room and down the stair. The house was very still. What if Jesus should come and find nobody awake? Would he go again and give them no presents? She couldn't expect any herself—but might he not let her take theirs for the rest? Perhaps she ought to wake them all, but she dared not without being sure.

On the last landing above the first floor, she saw, by the low gaslight at the end of the corridor, an unknown figure pass the foot of the stair: could she have anything to do with the marvel of the day? The woman looked up, and Phosy dropped the question. Yet she might be a charwoman, whose assistance the expected advent rendered necessary. When she reached the bottom of the stair she saw her disappearing in her step-mother's room. That she did not like. It was the one room into which she could not go. But, as the house was so still, she would search everywhere else, and if she did not find him, would then sit down in the hall and wait for him.

The room next the foot of the stairs, and opposite her step-mother's was the spare room, with which she associated ideas of state and grandeur: where better could she begin than at the guest-chamber? There!—Could it be? Yes!—Through the chink of the scarce-closed door she saw light. Either he was already there or there they were expecting him. From that moment she felt as if lifted out of the body. Far exalted above all dread, she peeped modestly in, and then entered. Beyond the foot of the bed, a candle stood on a little low table, but nobody was to be seen. There was a stool near the table: she would sit on it by the candle, and wait for him. But ere she reached it, she caught sight of something upon the bed that drew her thither. She stood entranced. —Could it be?— It *might* be. Perhaps he had left it there while he went into her mamma's room with something for her. — The loveliest of dolls ever imagined! She drew nearer. The light was low, and the shadows were many: she could not be sure what it was. But when she had gone close up to it, she concluded with certainty that it was in very truth a doll—perhaps intended for her—but beyond doubt the most exquisite of dolls. She dragged a chair to the bed, got up, pushed her little arms softly under it, and drawing it gently to her, slid down with it. When she felt her feet firm on the floor, filled with the solemn composure of holy awe she carried the gift of the child Jesus to the candle, that she might the better admire its beauty and know its preciousness. But the light had no sooner fallen upon it than a strange undefinable doubt awoke within her. Whatever it was, it was the very essense of loveliness—the tiny darling with its alabaster face, and its delicately modelled hands and fingers! A long nightgown covered the rest.—Was it possible?—Could it be?—Yes, indeed! it must be—it could be nothing else than a *real* baby! What a goose she had been! Of course it was baby Jesus himself!—for was not this his very own Christmas Day on which he was always born?—If she had felt awe of his gift before, what a grandeur of adoring love, what a divine dignity possessed her, holding in her arms the very child himself! One shudder of bliss passed through her, and in an agony of possession she clasped the baby to her great heart—then at once became still with the satisfaction of eternity, with the peace of God. She sat down on the stool, near the little table, with her back to the candle, that its rays should not fall on the eyes of the sleeping Jesus and wake him: there she sat, lost in the very majesty of bliss, at once the mother and the slave of the Lord Jesus.

She sat for a time still as marble waiting for marble to awake, heedful as tenderest woman not to rouse him before his time, though her heart was swelling with the eager petition that he would ask his Father to be as good as chasten her. And as she sat, she began, after her wont, to model her face to the like-ness of his, that she might understand his stillness— the absolute peace that dwelt on his countenance. But as she did so, again a sudden doubt invaded her: Jesus lay so very still—never moved, never opened his pale eye-lids! And now set thinking, she noted that he did not breathe. She had seen babies asleep, and their breath came and went—their little bosoms heaved up and down, and sometimes they would smile, and sometimes they would moan and sigh. But Jesus did none of these things: was it not strange? And then he was cold—oh, so cold!

A blue silk coverlid lay on the bed: she half rose and dragged it off, and contrived to wind it around herself and the baby. Sad at heart, very sad, but un-dismayed, she sat and watched him on her lap.

## CHAPTER VI

EANTIME the morning of Christmas Day grew. The light came and filled the house. The sleep-ers slept late, but at length they stirred. Alice awoke last—from a troubled sleep, in which the events of the night mingled with her own lost condition and destiny. After all Polly had been kind, she thought, and got Sophy up without disturbing her.

She had been but a few minutes down, when a strange and appalling rumour made itself—I cannot say audible, but—somehow known through the house, and every one hurried up in horrible dismay.

The nurse had gone into the spare room, and missed the little dead thing she had laid there. The bed was between her and Phosy, and she never saw her. The doctor had been sharp with her about some-thing the night before: she now took her revenge in suspicion of him, and after a hasty and fruitless visit of inquiry to the kitchen, hurried to Mr. Greatorex.

The servants crowded to the spare room, and when their master, incredulous indeed, yet shocked at the tidings brought him, hastened to the spot, he found them all in the room, gathered at the foot of the bed. A little sunlight filtered through the red window-curtains, and gave a strange pallid expression to the flame of the candle, which had now burned very low. At first he saw nothing but the group of servants, silent, motionless, with heads leaning forward, intently gazing: he had come just in time: another moment and they would have ruined the lovely sight. He stepped forward, and saw Phosy, half shrouded in blue, the candle behind illuminating the hair she had found too rebellious to the brush, and making of it a faint aureole about her head and white face, whence cold and sorrow had driven all the flush, rendering it colourless as that upon her arm which had never seen the light. She had pored on the little face until she knew death, and now she sat a speechless mother of sorrow, bending in the dim light of the tomb over the body of her holy infant.

How it was I cannot tell, but the moment her father saw her she looked up, and the spell of her dumbness broke.

"Jesus is dead," she said, slowly and sadly, but with perfect calmness. "He is dead," she repeated. "He came too early, and there was no one up to take care of him, and he's dead—dead—dead!"

But as she spoke the last words, the frozen lump of agony gave way; the well of her heart suddenly filled, swelled, overflowed; the last word was half sob, half shriek of utter despair and loss.

Alice darted forward and took the dead baby tenderly from her. The same moment her father raised the little mother and clasped her to his bosom. Her arms went round his neck, her head sank on his shoulder, and sobbing in grievous misery, yet already a little comforted, he bore her from the room.

"No, no, Phosy!" they heard him say. "Jesus is not dead, thank God. It is only your little brother that hadn't life enough, and is gone back to God for more."

Weeping, the women went down the stairs. Alice's tears were still flowing, when John Jephson entered. Her own troubles forgotten in the emotion of the scene she had just witnessed, she ran to his arms and wept on his bosom.

John stood as one astonied.

"O Lord! this *is* a Christmas!" he sighed at last.

"Oh John!" cried Alice, and tore herself from his embrace, "I forgot! You'll never speak to me again, John! Don't do it, John."

And with the words she gave a stifled cry, and fell a-weeping again, behind her two shielding hands.

"Why, Alice!—you ain't married, are you?" gasped John, to whom that was the only possible evil.

"No, John, and never shall be: a respectable man like you would never think of looking twice at a poor girl like me!"

Let's have one more look anyhow," said John, drawing her hands from her face. "Tell me what's the matter, and if there's anything can be done to right you, I'll work day and night to do it, Alice."

"There's nothing *can* be done, John," replied Alice, and would again have floated out on the ocean of her misery, but in spite of wind and tide, that is, sobs and tears, she held on by the shore at his entreaty, and told her tale, not even omitting the fact that when she went to the eldest of the cousins, inheriting through the misfortune of her and her brother so much more than their expected share, and "demeaned herself" to beg a little help for her brother, who was dying of consumption, he had all but ordered her out of the house, swearing he had nothing to do with her or her brother, and saying she ought to be ashamed to show her face.

"And that when we used to make mud pies together!" concluded Alice with indignation. "There John! you have it all," she added. "——And now?"

With the word she gave a deep, humbly questioning look into his honest eyes.

"Is that all, Alice?" he asked.

"Yes, John; ain't it enough?" she returned.

"More'n enough," answered John. "I swear to you, Alice, you're worth to me ten times what you would ha' been, even if you'd ha' had me, with ten thousand pounds in your ridicule. Why, my woman, I never saw you look one 'alf so 'an'some as you do now!"

"But the disgrace of it, John!" said Alice, hanging her head, and so hiding the pleasure that would dawn through all the mist of her misery.

"Let your father and mother settle that betwixt 'em, Alice. 'Tain't none o' my business. Please God, we'll do different.—When shall it be, my girl?"

"When you like, John," answered Alice, without raising her head, thoughtfully.

When she had withdrawn herself from the too rigorous embrace with which he received her consent, she remarked—

"I do believe, John, money ain't a good thing! Sure as I live, with the very wind o' that money, the devil entered into me. Didn't you hate me, John? Speak the truth now."

"No, Alice, I did cry a bit over you, though. You *was* possessed like."

"I *was* possessed. I do believe if that money hadn't been took from me, I'd never ha' had you, John. Ain't it awful to think on?"

"Well, no. O' coorse! How could ye?" said Jephson—with reluctance.

"Now, John, don't ye talk like that, for I won't

stand it. Don't you go for to set me up again with excusin' of me. I'm a nasty conceited cat, I am—and all for nothing but mean pride."

"Mind ye, ye're mine now, Alice; an' what's mine's mine, an' I won't have it abused. I knows you twice the woman you was afore, and all the world couldn't gi' me such another Christmas-box—no, not if it was all gold watches and roast beef."

When Mr. Greatorex returned to his wife's room, and thought to find her asleep as he had left her, he was dismayed to hear sounds of soft weeping from the bed. Some tone or stray word, never intended to reach her ear, had been enough to reveal the truth concerning her baby.

"Hush! hush!" he said, with more love in his heart than had moved there for many months, and therefore more in his tone than she had heard for as many;—"if you cry you will be ill. Hush, my dear!"

In a moment, ere he could prevent, she had flung her arms around his neck as he stooped over her.

"Husband, husband!" she cried, "is it my fault?"

"You behaved perfectly," he returned. "No woman could have been braver."

"Ah, but I wouldn't stay at home when you wanted me."

"Never mind that now, my child," he said.

At the word she pulled his face down to hers.

"I have *you*, and I don't care," he added.

"Do you care to have me?" she said, with a sob that ended in a loud cry. "Oh! I don't deserve it. But I *will* be good after this. I promise you I will."

"Then you must begin now, my darling. You must lie perfectly still, and not cry a bit, or you will go after the baby, and I shall be left alone."

She looked up at him with such a light in her face as he had never dreamed of there before. He had never seen her so lovely. Then she withdrew her arms, repressed her tears, smiled, and turned her face away. He put her hands under the clothes, and in a minute or two she was again fast asleep.

## CHAPTER VII

THAT day, when Phosy and her father had sat down to their Christmas dinner, he rose again, and taking her up as she sat, chair and all, set her down close to him, on the other side of the corner of the table. It was the first of a new covenant between them. The father's eyes having been suddenly opened to her character and preciousness, as well as to his own neglected duty in regard to her, it was as if a well of life had burst forth at his feet. And every day, as he looked in her face and talked to her, it was with more and more respect for what he found in her, with growing tenderness for her predilections, and reverence for the divine idea enclosed in her ignorance, for her childish wisdom, and her calm seeking—until at length he would have been horrified at the thought of training her up in *his* way: had she not a way of her own to go—following—not the dead Jesus, but Him who liveth for evermore? In the endeavour to help her, he had to find his own position towards the truth; and the results were weighty.—Nor did the child's influence work forward merely. In his intercourse with her he was so often reminded of his first wife, and that with the gloss or comment of a childish reproduction, that his memories of her at length grew a little tender, and through the child he began to understand the nature and worth of the mother. In her child she had given him what she could not be herself. Unable to keep up with him, she had handed him her baby, and dropped on the path.

Nor was little Sophy his only comfort. Through their common loss and her husband's tenderness,

Letty began to grow a woman. And her growth was the more rapid that, himself taught through Phosy, her husband no longer desired to make her adopt his tastes, and judge with his experiences, but, as became the elder and the tried, entered into her tastes and experiences—became, as it were, a child again with her, that, through the thing she was, he might help the thing she had to be.

As soon as she was able to bear it, he told her the story of the dead Jesus, and with the tale came to her heart love for Phosy. She had lost a son for a season, but she had gained a daughter for ever.

Such were the gifts the Christ-child brought to one household that Christmas. And the days of the mourning of that household were ended.

CORAGE, GOD MEND AL